ALSO BY GEORGE STEINER

The Death of Tragedy

In Bluebeard's Castle: Some Notes Toward the Redefinition of Culture

Tolstoy or Dostoevsky

Extraterritorial: Papers on Literature and the Language Revolution

Anno Domini

Language and Silence: Essays on Language, Literature and the Inhuman

After Babel: Aspects of Language and Translation

Martin Heidegger

On Difficulty and Other Essays

GEORGE STEINER

The Portage to San Cristóbal of A.H.

SIMON AND SCHUSTER / NEW YORK

A portion of this book appeared
in *The Kenyon Review* in 1979.

Published by Simon and Schuster
A Division of Gulf & Western Corporation
Simon & Schuster Building
Rockefeller Center
1230 Avenue of the Americas
New York, New York 10020
Originally published in Great Britain in 1981 by Faber and Faber Limited
SIMON AND SCHUSTER and colophon are trademarks of Simon & Schuster
Manufactured in the United States of America

3   4   5   6   7   8   9   10

Library of Congress Cataloging in Publication Data

Steiner, George, [date]
    The portage to San Cristóbal of A.H.
    I. Title.
PR6069.T417P6   1981   823'.914   82-829
ISBN 0-671-44572-3   AACR2

1

— You.

The very old man chewed his lip.

— You. Is it really? *Shema*. In God's Name. Look at you. Look at you now. You. The one out of hell.

And saying it the young man, almost a boy, tightened his calves and tried to drive his worn boots into the ground. To be implacable. But the voice shook inside him.

— It is you. Isn't it. We have you. We have you. Simeon is sending the signal. Everyone will know. The whole world. But not yet. We have to get you out of here. Ours. You are ours. You know that don't you. The living God. Into our hands. He delivered you into our hands. And it came to pass. You.

And the boy forced himself to laugh, but couldn't hear the echo. The still air lay between them, the rain shaking out of its hot, still folds.

— Silent now? Whose voice. They say your voice could.

The boy had never heard it.

— Burn cities. They say that when you spoke. Leaves turning

to ash and men weeping. They say that women, just to hear your voice, that women.

He stopped. The last woman they had seen was on the river-bank at Jiaro. Endless marches back. With no teeth. Squatting by the green pool and not waving to them.

— Would tear their clothes off, just to hear your voice.

And now the rage came. At last.

— Why don't you speak? Why don't you answer me? They'll make you speak. They'll tear it out of you. Ours. We have you. Thirty years hunting. Kaplan dead. And Weiss and Amsel. Oh you'll talk. Till we have the skin off you. The soulskin.

The boy was shouting now. Sucking at the air and shouting. The very old man looked up and blinked.

— *Ich?*

2

Ryder passed his fingers over the crack in the leather binding. The lot would have to be oiled again. The recollection of the day on which he bought that particular book came up sharp. At Wells, not far from the wide glory of the cathedral porch. In a shop as brown and fine-grained as the book itself. Then he turned from the shelves and walked to the window.

— Yes. Yes, I know they've been hunting for him. They've never stopped. Started almost immediately after the war. Small parties sworn to get him. To give their lives. Never to rest until he was found. And they've been at it since, I dare say. Lost some men doing it. That shooting business at Paraná. When was it? Late fifties, as I recall. That was when Amsel was killed. Oh it was never mentioned, of course. But some of your chaps saw him at São Paulo on the way in. One of the best of them, you know. Worked with us during the war. In and out of Poland. Twice, I believe. Trying to get Bomber Command to do something about the rail lines. Wanted me to go to the old man and tell him about the ovens. The old man wouldn't have believed

9

me you know. Not his kind of war really. So Amsel got out. Wishing us in hell, I imagine. After that he helped run the blockade. I wonder what went wrong at Paranā. He was frightfully good at his job. Alpha I'd say.

Ryder peered out the window. Though the delicate whorls and shadows of tower and lodge were as familiar to him as breath, he found it difficult to turn back to his two visitors. It struck him that their shoes looked oddly large in the light of the fire.

— As you say, Bennett, they've never believed either us or the Russians. Despite the dentures. They've always thought he decamped a few days before the bunker was surrounded. And that plane did take off, you know, with a passenger. We've got an eyewitness to that. It need not have been Bormann. No proof that he was in Berlin at the time. It could have been someone else. Never a trace of that plane. Anywhere. Just the testimony that it got away through the smoke, and turned south.

Evelyn Ryder was pacing now, rapidly, between the cabinet and the window, the curve of his high shadow brushing over the bookshelves.

— Mark you, I don't think there's much in it. I've been certain from the start. Almost certain. (Almost is a very good word, Ryder. It had been Strakes' last and only bit of advice before Ryder went off to give his first tutorial.) I don't think he wanted to get out. Not then. Not with the whole crazy thing blazing around him. Actor to the end. That's the secret of him, you know, mad keen on theater. Impresario, drama of history and all that. Supreme judge of an audience. Too great an artist in his own insane way to throw away that curtain. And I've gone over the evidence with a fine-tooth comb. Every bit of it. The Russians made off with the chauffeur and the doctor. Did them to death later so far as we know. But the identification looked pretty certain. And there are the teeth.

— We've only got one statement on that. The woman who said she had helped make the plate. I've got a report on her from Smithson. He didn't think she was all that much to go on.

— I know, Bennett, I know, but I'm inclined to believe she's telling the truth. All the evidence points that way. We've mapped his last days in detail. We can account for every hour. We know what he ate, whom he saw, when he last saw the sky. I can tell you when he went to the lavatory if you care to know. If he had really got away someone would have told us. Those that survived came up like frightened rats.

— But suppose

It was Hoving speaking, the younger of the two men who had come up from London on that autumn afternoon. He had not worked with Professor Ryder during the war.

— there was a double. That there was someone whom they wanted us to find in the Chancellery courtyard. It must have been hard enough to tell them apart when alive. If you had only the charred remains, bits of bone. How could you be sure?

— We thought of that. I kept turning it over in my mind. Just possible, of course. But this whole business of a double. Very interesting, I don't deny it. But little we really know about it. Bennett will correct me on this, but there were only two occasions on which we had any real evidence that a double was being used. In Prague once, and then in the last year, during one of those hospital visits on the eastern front. I've thought about the man. Oh interminably. Tried to get inside a bit of his skin as it were. And I don't see it. Using a double at that point, where it mattered so that the ghastly show be done right. The high note and Valhalla. And how could he be that sure of any other human being, leaving another man to step into his own fire? When everything around him was betrayal.

— He thought he would come back, didn't he? That the Reich would rise again if only he could survive, make his voice heard.

— Quite so. I remember when we first talked about that, Bennett. Just before I went out to look at the stuff. The Barbarossa dream. The storm king in the mountain lair. And out for vengeance when his people call. He may have believed that

11

sometimes. But not at the last. I don't suppose he wanted time to go on, not after him. And history and the cities and the chosen race were to perish with him. In the last fire. Sardanapalus. There's a lot of that in German romantic poetry, you know. And he was a romantic. A romantic mountebank. Mad to the heart but with a brightness —

Ryder stopped, embarrassed. *Le mot juste*. But not exactly. Rather than search for it, he glanced over at Bennett. How Bennett had aged since the war. How heavy the skin lay under his eyes. In that instant Ryder felt the whole of his own body. Time had dealt more lightly with it. He stretched his arm to pour the sherry.

— Are you sure about that signal? Have you got the code right?

He went back to his desk and peered again at the small sheet of blue paper with its familiar blazons of high secrecy.

— As you know, sir,

It was Hoving.

— we've been following the operation for some time. And picked up a fair number of messages as they went upriver. We're pretty sure we've got the cipher right. Not a very difficult one, actually. In fact, I'd say it was almost too easy. As if they didn't care who listened in. A Concordance to the Old Testament and a pretty elementary set of permutations. We've got a local chap, in Orosso, one of the last airstrips. A man called Kulken. He's been listening in steadily. Their transmitter isn't much. Signals have been getting weaker. Of course, there is the weather there. Pure hell I'd imagine. Clouds never off the ground and the wet eating through your wires. No one really knows. No white man that is. So far as we can tell there's never been a party beyond the falls. They call them the Chevaqua falls: the waters of boiling teeth. And they're a thousand miles from nowhere.

— Yes, but this particular message. Garbled.

— Quite. But not hard to reconstruct.

Bennett reached over for it and read slowly.

— First word indecipherable. Then: Praise be to Him. Thou art remembered O Jerusalem. It looks as if the first word was a short one. Monosyllable, I'd say.

— Found.

Ryder was startled at the sharpness of his own voice.

— Yes, I should have thought so. Found.

And Bennett folded the paper and slipped it back in his waist-coat pocket. Sir Evelyn Ryder drummed his fingers against the decanter. The cool exact feel of the glass flattered him.

— It's a pretty queer business, I'll grant you that. And just possible. Just. Million-to-one shot. I'm certain in my own mind that we know what happened. He shot himself in that warren of his and they burned the holy remains in the yard. As fast as they knew how. With the shells detonating all around them. I've never thought that plane could have got very far. The sky was like a furnace in those last days. And I just don't believe he was on it. Not his style. No, Bennett, if you ask me, I don't think the thing is on. They've been tracking down other men out there. Minor butchers. All the chaps that were at Wannsee when the Jewish question was settled. We never laid hands on the half of them. I dare say they've found *somebody*. Very likely it's some-one important. Dietrichsen or Sepner or Pirveč, the insane devil who came into Carinthia in '43. And good luck to them. But *him*? I shouldn't have thought so.

The three men were on their feet, their shadows tinged by the reddening coal.

— But you will keep me posted won't you? Anything you pick up. I'm anxious to know. It brings back the old days, doesn't it, Bennett. You remember that balls-up in Tunis. I thought they'd have our hide for that.

The slow chimes were ringing for hall. Ryder was halfway into his gown, when he stopped.

— That point you made earlier, Hoving. Suppose

His fine-boned features opened to an expression of gross enchantment.

13

— that the one they've caught is the double. Yes. Yes. Don't you see it? The poor devil looked so like his master that he wouldn't dare be captured. No one would believe him. He had to get away. To the ends of the earth. If they've got someone it's the shadow, the mask of him. Who must be very old now. And how can *they* believe him? Having crawled a thousand miles through that green hell to fetch him out. If that's what's happened, Bennett, I'd say —

And they started down the spiral staircase.

3

Simeon bit at his broken nail and tasted oil. The anatomy of transistors and close-threaded wires lay before him intricately hurt. The delicate beast corroded by the incessant damp, until its voice had dimmed to an unsteady croak under the larger voice of the rain. He braided the wire around the bent screw, but where the insulation was gone the metal itself seemed to sweat under a fine web of decay. Bending close over the set he could see the spreading life of the fungus. He had cleaned the circuit boards a dozen times over. Now the soldering came apart in his sweating fingers. He turned his shoulders slightly to get out of Benasseraf's near shadow.

— Did you get through?

— I think so. I'm not sure. There's almost no juice. Look at the wiring here. Rotten all the way through.

— But you think they picked up the signal?

— I hope so. I can't be certain. Look for yourself. Turn the crank

Simeon bent close listening for the voice of the broken thing.

— and nothing happens. Dead. I don't think I can patch it again. But something did get through. It must have. Part of it at least.

— If I forget thee O Jerusalem.

The words sang under Benasseraf's breath.

— They *must* have heard us. If we're to get him out alive. If they didn't get your signal, there'll be no one to get us out. They've heard us, Simeon. The plane will be in San Cristóbal. To fly us home. To fly. After the years of walking. Lieber will be there to meet us. He knows now. That we've found him. My God, Simeon, we've found him.

But Simeon wasn't listening. Not after the word Lieber. It brought back to him, with a pressure sudden and more blurring than the rawness of his sweating face, the notion of a world beyond the clearing, beyond the barbed, dripping wall of trees. Emmanuel Lieber, whose fingers they were, often fumbling and ten thousand miles from his arm's length, but his as surely as if he were now standing with them, dreaming the web, spinning and tightening it over the grid of the jungle, directing their racked, unbelieving bodies to the quarry, as he had for thirty years from London, then from Turin (where they had first, in worlds past it seemed, picked up the scent) and now from the small, unmarked office in Lavra Street in Tel Aviv. They were his creatures, the animate embers of his calm, just madness. Of a will so single, so inviolate to any other claim of life, that its thread went through Lieber's sleep producing one incessant dream. That of this capture. Emmanuel Lieber in San Cristóbal, waiting at the landing strip which they had hacked out of the lianas and then covered over with brush and vine leaves. Waiting to fly them out, the lost hunters and their game. An image almost absurd, because of the silence, the necessary absence of Lieber's person and the loud waste of the jungle. There was next to nothing left of Emmanuel Lieber when he crawled out from under the burnt flesh in the death pit of Bialka. And he had never taken the time to mend, so that his will raged visible beneath the

16

gray, splotched skin, and behind the thick glasses. Yet he was beautiful. Simeon remembered that now and was startled. His eyes. Marked by the things seen. As if the fires at Bialka, the children hung alive, the bird droppings glistening on the shorn heads of the dying, had filled Lieber's eyes with a secret light. No, that was kitsch. Not a secret light. But a perception so outside the focus of man's customary vision had given Lieber's broken features and low voice, and the shy rigor of his motions, a piercing strangeness. The stench went from Lazarus but even long after no one could take their eyes from him.

Beyond Lieber and San Cristóbal waited the great tumult of voices, of those who would soon hear the news and not believe.

— Found him, Simeon. Found him.

Now he looked at Benasseraf and the dead weight of the radio transmitter came back into his shoulders. Yes, they had found him. But the shock of the last hours was too new. And the memory of the near abandonments. First when Stroessner's hooligans had drawn Amsel into a death trap at Paraná. Then when a whole squad of hunters (my dervishes, said Lieber) had disappeared, almost without human trace, in the swamplands south of the Cordilla Nera. Was his the last party left? Simeon was no longer certain. And what of their own surrenders, of the innumerable times they had resolved to turn back, doubting, deriding the quiet mania of Lieber's conviction? Only a year ago, not five hundred miles in from the coast, when Father Girón had explained to them, speaking out of the knowledge of his own skin, parchment yellow and bruised by countless journeys, that no man, be he devil's spawn, could live in the unmapped quicksand and green bogs beyond the falls. And a hundred times after that. Nearly every day. When Benasseraf fell ill in the encampment at the headwaters of the Bororo and danced in the heat of his fever. When the rains, black stampedes of water, swept away their supplies, split their boots open as with rat's teeth and all but lashed the clothing off their backs. When the maps went mute.

17

As they did about two hundred miles south-southwest of Jiaro. Where cartographers had marked, with pale blue strokes and wavelets, a blank of uncharted swampland. No man could live beyond the falls, in the quaking marsh and sulfurous air. So said Father Girón, and the Chava Indians who had watched them pass with hungry derision. But had lent them a guide, a hollow-ribbed heron of a creature who could throw slivers of bark on to the green scum of the morass and tell where there was footing.

Perhaps that had been the nearest point to rout. When, only ten days ago, yet it seemed to Simeon much much longer, the Indian had melted away from them, refusing to wade a step farther into the stinking water, his mouth set with panic. And the five of them had stood, up to the armpits in the green heat of the living mud, the swamp sucking at their blistered skins like the pale-bellied leeches. They had stood single file, trying to hold their packs above their heads, the midges swarming at their swollen eyelids. And Simeon knew that if he faced about, if he turned his shoulders under the suffocating canvas of dead, poisoned air, they would turn back, to Jiaro, and the crossing of the Cordillera and the wonder of cold beer and open sky that waited at San Cristóbal. The next step had been everything. Hosannah, though he had almost fallen into the shifting ooze and his bones had frozen at the sudden slither of the snake. He had taken that step because Lieber was at his back. Whose voice, as they read the cipher, insisted, with an insistence deeper, more binding than even the swamp, that the man was in there, that this was his lair and desolation, that another thirty miles.

They had crawled those thirty miles. Inchwise. On their knees and with loosening bowels. Until the clearing, and the point of light. The insect-swarming oil lamp in his window.

— Yes. We've found him. Praise be to God and peace on our souls.

But as he said it and reached out to touch Benasseraf's hand, Simeon knew that he was deceiving himself. About the exhaustions and physical barriers that had so nearly made them turn back. It had not been Amsel's death, or the disappearance of Kaplan, or the hideousness of jungle and swamp. These things had made them maniacs and browned skeletons. But the true obstacle, each of them carrying it inside himself like hidden leprosy, was far greater. Indifference. Common sense with its fine sharp bite. A boredom with vengeance so acute that it rose in them, during the fever marches or stinging nights, like the taste of vomit. So what? Even if he is alive. Why drag the aged swine out of this stretch of hell? Who cares, now, thirty years after, or is it more? We're doing his bidding here, emptying our lives in this stinking jungle when we could be building, when we could be knitting ourselves new and forgetting. No one cares any more. Even if we find him alive, if we get him out, who'll want the stinking carcass? And what will they do to him? He's no more than a poisonous ghost now, and we're mad to hunt him down. Mad as he is. Exactly what is it he did to man? What is it they say he did? Who will be left alive to remember?

They had not spoken these sentences aloud. Not since they had taken the oath just before their ship sailed from Genoa, Lieber touching each one of them on the forehead and then lost in the crowd at the bottom of the gangplank. To find him, be it at the cost of their lives. Not to return until they had found him or had absolute proof that he was dead. Simeon remembered the plangent tumult of Italian partings. And John Asher, next to him at the railing, saying: Immigrants, like ourselves. We're immigrants out of life.

So they had not said any of these things out loud. But had thought them so intensely, with such deepening bitterness, that Simeon could make out each question, doubt, crisis of self-mockery or forgetting, in their sleeping faces, in their rebellious stumbling, in the rages that had all but torn them apart during the final year of the chase.

— It was time we did. High time.

Benasseraf eased the strap on his sweat-blackened shirt and

nodded. It seemed to Simeon that they had spoken very little of late. All of them. As if they were afraid of the poisoned gnats that might enter their mouths. But he was trying to get the thing clear, those last hours and the capture. As Lieber had dreamt it. It was in his dream that they had moved, in the insane, unwavering certitude of Lieber's dream. Right to the edge of the clearing.

They had stumbled on it at twilight, the sudden break of sky over the circle of charred stumps. And crouched at the rim, in the insect-loud grass, like men overwhelmed. They had crouched the whole night through, their bones knotted by the cold breath of the swamp. Not saying a word. Their thoughts numb at the fantastic nearness of the end. Believing Lieber now, yet unable to believe that he had actually mapped this minute rent in the forest, that he had drawn this last small circle around the man, unraveling the sinuous logic of his successive flights, deeper and deeper into the interior, from one foul cover to the next. They had crouched there till the sour note of a tucca bird signaled the dim, wet rise of day. Two men had come out of the hut. An old man, one-armed and in a gray tunic, and a much younger, dark-faced guard, carrying a fowling piece, which he pointed vaguely at the sky before sitting down.

Isaac Amsel, to whom the enterprise had become a vengeance too narrow, too selfish, and whom they had tried to send back since first he hung around them in the marshaling yard at São Paulo, rushed forward, against Simeon's order. And fired. So that the sound of the shot rebounded in an absurd, thunderous echo from the green wall of the forest. The guard had risen, spun histrionically and fallen dead. What had killed the other man as he scratched at the thin bed of lettuce was not clear. Fright, perhaps, or the end of the long wait.

They had raced across the open ground, each momentarily lost to the others. Mindless of Lieber's warnings, of the curare-tipped staves which they found outside the abode in the Sangra

20

cañon, of the trip wires and antipersonnel mines sown around the first bunker, his opulent lair in the hills above Paraná.

There had in fact been a wire, and Asher tripped over it. But it ended in a pit of sodden leaves, the firing pin long since rotten.

Beyond Benasseraf's heavy breathing, the fever was often at him, Simeon could hear the click of the spade. Striking the patch of gravel which was the lone bit of solid ground in the waterlogged clearing. They were burying the old gardener and the man with the gun. There was no ammunition. They knew that now. He had spent the last shot, long ago perhaps, on the marmots and rubber-bellied lizards whose bluish bones they had found behind the stove.

Simeon and Benasseraf walked over to the grave. Asher was smoothing down the broken grass and gray mud. The grave was shallow and Simeon could make out the contour of the guard's foot. It was slightly deformed and where the spade had struck the toes had come wide apart. He could not take his eyes off the vague shape and it filled his mind with ugly, tattered images. They cut across the film of sweat which seemed to close around him at every motion and the raw edge of the transmitter pressing on the small of his back. Asher looked up.

— Did you get through, Capitano?

— I think so. Not the whole of it. But enough to let them know.

He wanted to explain about the transmitter and the corroded generator coils. But Elie Barach had begun his prayers for the dead. Had stepped back from the hurried pit and begun the rise and fall of his prayer. Over the months of heat and jungle drippings, the forest sticking to them like resin, Barach's cap had become a blacker patch in the tangled blackness of his hair. The morning shone through his threadbare shawl and his body swayed gently with the words. His eyes were closed and he appeared to move outward with the tide of his prayer, easily, being so light a guest in his own flesh.

— And may You take their souls into Your keeping. And give rest unto those who had none upon earth. May they find peace who brought none. And forgiveness who so need it. Amen.

But the prayer began anew.

— For Thou alone art judge. Thine is the vengeance and Thine the pardon. It behooves not us. It is not ours. Guard us, O Lord, from the temptations of righteousness. Guard us from certitude. From dealing in Thy Name when that Name, hallowed be it, is a secret beyond secrets. *Selah.* From doing Thy will when we know it not. Or only, O God, such small part of it. Make us Thine instrument but not Thy replacers. For we stand in exceeding peril. We who have striven so long that we have become our single purpose. Who are less than we were because Thou hast given us beyond our deserving. Do not ask of us, O Lord, that we do vengeance or show mercy. The task is greater than we are. It passes understanding. And whom Thou hast now delivered into our hands, may he be Thine utterly. Amen.

— Yes, said Simeon,

— They must have picked up our call. Can you imagine Lieber. In this hour, when he knows.

— If we manage to get him out. To bring him out alive.

And Asher repeated it, giving a last tug at his spade.

If he did it a little less well, thought Benasseraf, if the words were a little less round. Like the gold coins when we dug up the jar in Caesarea.

Elie passed his hands over his moist forehead and smiled, still in the wake of his prayer.

— We'll get him out. If we have to carry him. Every stinking mile.

Benasseraf spoke loudly.

— Just as we said in our oath. With our lives if need be. We'll hand him over to Lieber. If he has to ride on our backs to get there.

— That might be the only way.

22

Asher said it brushing the rust-gray hair out of his eyes.

— Because I don't see him walking. Not far. He's an old man now. I thought of that last night, when we were in the grass, freezing our balls off. Born in 1889. That's it, isn't it? It says so on Lieber's warrant. I remembered that last night. Walk through the swamp, at his age?

— And over the moraine, said Elie.

— And how strong do you think he is? I mean, look at what they've been eating. Mice and raw beans and lots of muck scratched off the trees. We'll be lucky if we can *carry* him out alive. He shakes, even out here in the sun.

He said it without looking back at the hut.

— Ninety years old. That's as old as he is. Men and women ninety years old. The crippled and the blind and the ones spitting blood. They made them walk barefoot, over the cobbles. And whoever fell behind, they threw water over their feet. So that they would freeze to the stones. And stand there till they died. Burning alive in their skins. At Chelmno, there was a rabbi, a man of wonders. A hundred years old. And they tore out his tongue

Benasseraf brought his hands to his mouth.

— and made him hold it before him, and walk. A mile. More than that. Till he came to the fire pit. And they told him: Sing. Sing you man of wonder.

He went on picturing the device in his own mind.

— When he can't walk, we'll carry him. In a litter. We can use one of the hammocks and tie it between two poles. We'll put a poncho on top to keep his carcass dry. We'll take turns carrying him. Like the ark.

— And dance before it, said Asher.

— Are you being serious, Ben? Carry a man through the swamp, when we can barely keep our heads above the filth? And Elie is right. What of the rockfall? Most of our ropes are gone. Swept down the bloody falls or torn to shreds. It can take

23

hours to go a hundred yards in that stinging hell. Imagine trying to get a hammock through. He isn't all that light. There's a paunch on the bleeding old ghost. No. We need help. And fast.

Simeon looked up at Asher, entranced, as so often, by his sober fantasies.

— They've got to get supplies to us. Blankets, guy ropes, Benzedrine, iodine, crampons, a new transmitter, we could do with two more sleeping bags, batteries are rotten in two of the flashlights, quinine. The lot. We need cocoa and fishing lines. I've got one decent lure left. And we could do with more fuel for the Primus. I say we wait here, until they drop some of the stuff. And skirt the swamp. I don't know that we can get ourselves back through that ordure, let alone carry the old devil. Track along the western edge, until we find open ground. I don't think we can make San Cristóbal. Not in a month of Sundays. It's all very well on Lieber's map. Red arrow in and blue arrow out. He hasn't been here. He hasn't seen the poisonous muck. Or the Chavas. If we try to slog out there won't be enough left of our bones to fill a matchbox. Look here, Capo, you try and get a supply drop, and then we can make it to the scrub. And wait till they lift us out. Or ferry him at least. Look at the rabbi's boots. I can see his bleeding corns.

Elie smiled and shifted his foot.

— We'd be mad to try. Stark raving mad. And he'd die on us inside a week. Turn over and die like a bloated water rat. They owe us that much. I mean we've found him, haven't we? Found him alive at the bottom of nowhere. The four of us and that nit. Why shouldn't they get us out? Helicopters, medics, the whole shooting match. To drown in that hell bog? After all this. After we've gone and dug him up alive. Or freeze to death on the bloody col? I won't do it.

— Even if I can get the transmitter working

Elie leaned forward and interrupted Simeon.

— they won't come for us. No one will. Perhaps Emmanuel

24

will be waiting in San Cristóbal. Perhaps he won't even be there. We don't know that he's still alive. That his life has outlasted our news. There was only one thing left of him: his waiting. That was his soul and nerve and bone. Just like this man. Waiting. He too must have known that we would find him, someday, when he closed his eyes for an instant at the bottom of his warren. Two men will know that Simeon was not lying when he sent his message. He and Lieber. Who else will believe us? Even if they remember, why should they believe that the dead come to life, and in a hammock yet, carried out of the jungle. Even before we left they thought Emmanuel was sick in the head, that he had death and ashes in his brain. They wouldn't give him any help. Our own people. "Stop it, Lieber. Stop telling ghost stories. The beast is dead. Those rumors from the Chaco, those spoors in Paraguay, the telephoto bought from Major Gómez—and at what a staggering price, dear Lieber—all journalist's gossip. Trash. Someone trying to make a fool of us or start a diplomatic incident. Look what it's got us. Amsel murdered. The best agent we had. A professional, Lieber, and no offense meant. Murdered in a mousetrap. And for what? A wild whisper, a map which is probably a fake. Stop haunting us. Stop waiting outside our offices. We won't back you another inch. Not a penny. No more false papers and consular immunities. *Genug,* Emmanuel. If you find any men left *meshugge* enough to believe you, to go out there on a fool's errand, we don't want to know about it. If they die, their blood be on your head." That's what they said to Lieber. In the Ministry, at Military Intelligence, wherever he turned. "You're crazy, Lieber. Get out of the sun." If Emmanuel got our message, if he's still alive, he will meet us. His boots may be shabbier than mine. But he'll meet us. The others. May God wake them.

Asher caught the note of invocation:—and flay them alive.

Simeon marked the words pouring out after the long quiet. Gideon Benasseraf, John Asher, Elie Barach. Taking on their

25

own shapes again in the better light of late morning. He spoke slowly, making them draw near.

— It isn't that. Or it wouldn't be now. There *would* be help. And a helicopter coming in as far as Jiaro. If the news could be released. Oh if everyone knew, there'd be an airfield dug here, bigger than Lod. And roads bulldozed. And a million television cameras. And a Hilton. They wouldn't believe us, not at first, and not all of them. But if they heard his voice and we described just what he looks like, they'd come like locusts. And take him from us. That's the whole point. They'd take him to New York or Moscow or Nuremberg. And we'd be lucky if they allowed us to stand in the anteroom peering over a million heads. That's how it is in the museum, at Auschwitz. "Here perished the heroic Polish combatants against Fascism. Here the vanguard of the heroic Communist partisans were executed." And then in the corner: "Eighty Jewish women from the Warsaw Postal Service were deported here and died." *Eighty.* No. He'd be theirs to try, or parade around the world, or pension off. They wouldn't let us near him. We'd have waded up to our eyes in the filth and death of this place so that *they* could take him out. That's what Lieber fears most. And he's right. That story about the man and the large fish. The largest ever. But the sharks hammering at it, stripping it to the bone before he could reach the dock. If we call for help, if Lieber went to the Ministry and they were to send planes to get us out, or drop supplies, everyone would know. From São Paulo to Lima. And swarm at us. To take him away, to kick us onto the garbage heap. "Now we take over. This is too big for you to handle. Much too big. Mr. Hurok will handle it. And the International Court. We might call you to say your piece. Or we might not. Off with you now. No loitering." Eighty women. Subtract eighty from six million, and what do you get? Zero. The mathematics of the *goy. This* is the time when we must move fast, and keep most silent, and be secret to all. Don't you see? Until we have him home. Then go to the four corners of the city and blow your trumpets. But not

26

now. If they knew we had him, if they could follow us in here, they wouldn't leave us his shadow.

Simeon looked up, with sudden comfort, at the steaming mist.

— The way we came? There must be another way. We won't get out alive. Not any of us.

— I haven't had time to think about it, Gideon. There may be another route. At least for part of the way.

He unfolded the map from its waterproof case.

— But not at the start. The swamp is everywhere around us. That's why he came here. Because no man could follow. Except through the black water and the quicksand. He crouched in the dead center, on this mud bank, and we've got to wade through the thing if we want to get out.

— Bleeding Jesus. I'd rather rot here.

Asher's terminology, and the rich variants on it, always brought an elfin, secret expression to Elie Barach's face.

— Look for yourself. There's no other way. And after that we've got to reach Jiaro and see what we can dig up of our stores. I've left some spare circuit boards there, and wiring.

— Supper for termites, said Asher.

Simeon was bending over the map.

— But after Jiaro there *might* be an easier way. If we could turn the falls on the north side and avoid that portage. Here. About half a degree south of the Querracho. Do you remember what Girón said? That there was some kind of very large ruin in the valley. A lost city. Known to the Indians, and bits of it seen from the air. There was thought to be a road leading from it, stone slabs laid down by the Mayanos and leading to the quarries, to the bluestone quarries here, just above Orosso. If there's any kind of paving, it'll be easier to get through. And if we have to carry him—

— Isn't there a landing strip at Orosso?

Benasseraf pointed at the faintly drawn propeller in the middle of the green hatchings.

— I think so. Probably used by surveyors. But Lieber warned us not to use it. We'd be seen there. And we wouldn't have the range to fly out. It's got to be San Cristóbal.

— That means the mountains, and as he said it, Barach swayed on his heels.

— The rockfall, and the two pitches below the col. Without crampons or axes. And carrying the old swine on our backs. You're mad.

Simeon nodded, puzzled by his own gaiety, by the delight he took in Asher's rebellious good sense.

— We'll rest up somewhere outside Orosso. Perhaps there's another track. To the right of the glacier. Perhaps we don't need to go as high. And once we're over that

His finger straightened out to touch San Cristóbal. Though the easy unbending was a lie. The breadth of his oil-blackened nail covered ten thousand steps. The shadow of his finger spanned interminable hours hacking through jungle, thick as leather, and marching through the razor grass of the uplands. The map was an ambush, set to catch dreams. Extended eastward from the swamp his hand reached well into the blue void of the South Pacific, into safety and the long flight home. It should not be so easy to place a hand across a map where our feet must follow. An hour of sweat and fear to a thousandth of an inch.

— we're almost in reach. One or two of us can go ahead to contact Lieber. You and the boy. We'll see. Once we're off the mountains.

— The soulskin.

The word was so loud and ludicrous that the four men started up from the map and turned to look at the hut. Isaac Amsel saw them staring at him, flushed, and stepped back from his prisoner.

Simeon folded the map carefully, cradled the transmitter against his back and walked slowly toward the door of the hut. The others followed. He had not yet looked at the man. Not directly. He knew he would have to now. In his throat the air seemed to

28

close like a fist. The sweat lay cold and prickly at the corners of his mouth. He was near to gagging, but bound himself tight lest he make some stupid, irremediable gesture.

The old man had been looking at the boy. Seeing Simeon's shadow lengthen toward him he turned. And raised his head. Simeon choked. The caged air hammered at his ribs. He saw the man's eyes. For the first time. He saw the gray-green pupils under the puffed lids and the vein which rimmed them like a livid thread. The eyes were dead. But suddenly, in the cold ash, a minute, sharp crystal of light blazed. Then the gray smoke passed again over the man's glance. But in that instant Simeon found breath. The voice sprang out of him harsh and pent-up. The words spoke him and he trembled.

— AUFSTEHEN. LOS. I have a warrant here. Born April 20, 1889. In the name of man. For crimes herein listed. In the face of God. AUFSTEHEN. We're starting out. We're starting now. To take you home, Herr Hitler.

4

Because it had been a long time, a very long time, since he had traveled in an official car, and because his early-morning cigarette had a tart, pleasant edge, Nikolai Maximovitch Gruzdev had forgotten his fear. Or folded it somewhere in the back of his mind, away from the brilliance of the windows flashing by in the morning sun and the epaulets of his escort. The fear came back as they passed under the sudden bar of shadow at the gates. But it was not wholly unpleasant, and ascending in the silent lift, Nikolai Maximovitch felt his bowels shift comfortably.

Offices had not changed very much since his day, but the file cabinets were of a much improved model and there were two vases with flowers on the windowsill. Both men rose, momentarily cutting out the morning brightness, and even across the wide desk Gruzdev could smell the prickling scent of shaving lotion. His mind dwelt on that for an instant. Then he realized, with embarrassment, that he was meant to sit down.

The desk was heaped with dossiers. But their bright plastic tabs were entirely different from those he had known.

— It was good of you to come, Nikolai Maximovitch,

The shorter man spoke first.

— so early in the morning. I regret the inconvenience. The matter is of no great importance.

— No. I understand. Of course.

The moment he said these words, not knowing why he had spoken, and realizing how inept, how damaging they might prove, Gruzdev felt afraid. It was an abrupt fear near to panic. Worse than any he had known since the first afternoon of the interrogation. But the short man, only his shoulders seemed impressive, went on as if nothing had been said.

— A few small details. Matters of history. We are historians here, Nikolai Maximovitch. Bookworms. All these mountains of paper.

He swept his hand delicately over the desk.

— From time to time we try to do a housecleaning. To put a period to things. That is what historians should do. Put to rest. Do you agree?

The fear had ebbed. Gruzdev lit a fresh cigarette and inhaled. He did not do that often. Not before lunch.

— That is an interesting way of putting it. I agree, Comrade Colonel. Naturally.

— Where there is untidiness we must sometimes go back over things. Small things.

— Yes. The small things.

Colonel Shepilov looked at his visitor. But Gruzdev was staring past him, at the lit, cloudless sky. And thinking. Why is it so like Gogol? All such interviews. Even when death is very near. Everyone speaks as if they were quoting Gogol. The wonder of it carried his mind back. During the journey, and after, he had clung to the thought. It would all end bearably because Gogol had imagined it far ahead. They were merely acting it

31

out. *The small things*. It was a quotation, of course. But from which tale? He would look it up, as soon as he got home.

— As I said, Nikolai Maximovitch, it is good of you to come and assist us. In one or two small points. Please feel at ease. The sun is very bright this morning. The light. I trust it does not inconvenience you.

Shepilov riffled his papers and paused, his thumb bearing heavily on the margin of a photostat.

— There are a few details we should like to verify. In the testimony you gave. Particularly before the interrogations.

— But that was thirty years ago, Comrade Colonel. My memory is no longer of the best.

Gruzdev said it not because it was relevant, but because it seemed the proper form.

— We understand that. But the file is here. I have your signature before me. It is quite plain.

And he turned to the other man, who was a good deal taller than he, wore a brown suit and sometimes drew a handkerchief from his breast pocket to wipe the corner of his mouth.

— Tell us, Nikolai Maximovitch, why were you so certain? We are historians, not psychologists. We are puzzled. Your certitude interests us greatly.

— I was wrong, said Gruzdev. Surely that too is in your file. I was utterly mistaken. And made a full statement of my errors. You will find it in the court records. If you will allow me, Comrade Colonel

But he did not reach out toward the desk.

— Even after the two confrontations with Mengershausen. Even after SS Adjutant Rattenhuber confirmed to you, in front of witnesses, that Hitler and the woman Braun had killed themselves, that he had helped burn their bodies. Here is a transcript of your interview with Heinz Linge, Hitler's valet. Your initials are at the right-hand lower corner of each page, Nikolai Maximovitch. "Linge is in error. I continue to believe that the body

32

shown me by Captain Fyodor Pavlovich Vassiliki on May 11th last is not that of Adolf Hitler.'' And there is more of this.

Shepilov's fingers tugged at a bundle of foolscap.

— Yes. Here is the testimony of SS man Otto Guensche. A remarkable witness. He had helped carry the bodies into the yard. And what do I read here. ''Dr. Nikolai Maximovitch Gruzdev affirms that the said Otto Guensche is lying or mistaken.'' Your certitude, Gruzdev. It puzzles me.

— Comrade Colonel, I beg to observe

The voice was flat and servile. They had all acquired it, whether tenor or bass, during the interrogations. It bound them together however diverse their natural tones. Hearing it again in his own mouth, the last syllable of each word overstressed, Gruzdev flinched. He had not known that that voice remained in his throat, packed away with its echoes of pain and humiliation, but so ready for use.

— I beg to observe that all the denials you refer to, all my erroneous depositions, occurred during the preliminary inquiries. Indeed, the extent of my confusion is shown by the improper designation I then gave to witness Rattenhuber. The rank was not adjutant but *Brigadenführer*. I feel certain, Comrade Colonel, that the matter was corrected in my later statements.

Suddenly he realized that he remembered every detail. Like sharp pebbles in a shoe. His memory had betrayed him with a fierce precision. It would not mend, though ten years had passed since his return from the camp. Gruzdev felt sweat itching under his thin beard.

— You withdrew all these statements subsequently. That is correct. You concurred unreservedly in the findings of the official tribunal: to wit, that the bodies of Hitler and the woman Braun had been identified beyond any possible doubt by Captain Vassiliki and dental mechanic Fritz Echtmann. Asked to give reasons for your earlier obstinacy, you admitted that propaganda originating from Western intelligence services had infiltrated

General Chuikov's staff and your own department. The fullness of your testimony and the completeness of your retraction were taken into account when sentence was passed.

— Is all this necessary, Comrade Colonel?

The question had seemed unanswerable, even to himself, when it came from Gruzdev's bloodstained mouth during the last of the interrogations, and innumerable times thereafter, in the trains and in the Arctic clearing. Why ask it again? But Shepilov seemed pleased, as if some prefatory, laborious rite of courtesy had been absolved.

— No. It is, as you say Nikolai Maximovitch, unnecessary. We are busy men, you and I, not children. Your later testimony, your recantations, the report you submitted on Fascist influences in the official American war history

Shepilov's palm brushed idly over the green-covered notebook, the child's exercise book in which Gruzdev had written his additional confessions in the fourth winter at Vorkuta, and seeing it there, so casually naked, as had been his brain and body under the lights of the barrack, Gruzdev felt a hammering in his throat. He couldn't speak. Not without crying out.

— all these things are not of much concern to us now. The illegality of certain proceedings is, unfortunately, quite plain. The persuasions used to make you change your mind . . . but surely there is no need to go into that. To remember certain things too well is wasteful. What interests us now

Shepilov bent forward for the first time, shifting out of the direct brilliance of the morning light.

— is your reasons at the start. Before you were questioned by Major Berkoff and his assistants. What made you so certain that Hitler was alive, that all the evidence submitted to your medical judgment was inadequate? "The documents as enumerated above, together with my own examination, suggest to me that the evidence points to a very different conclusion." These are your own words, Comrade Doctor, recorded by the secretary of the commission of preliminary investigation on June 17th.

34

Who was the man in the brown suit? Trying to remember, Gruzdev frowned.

— These matters happened some years ago. We understand that. But the Historical Commission attaches importance to your present answers. Bear that in mind.

Why *had* he been so certain?

— I must ask the Comrade Colonel to remember that Stalin himself believed that Hitler had survived. He stated at the Potsdam conference that Hitler was being sheltered by Fascism in Spain or Latin America. When Major Berkoff informed me that Stalin had changed his mind, my last doubts were resolved.

The informing had been graphic. It burned still, when the weather changed, in Gruzdev's knit fingers. Sometimes it went through his kidneys like a long needle.

— There is no need to extend this inquiry beyond our competence. It is your reasons, not Stalin's, that concern us. Please feel free to continue smoking.

Gruzdev's cigarette had gone out. Why had he been so certain? Even after the first beating. It puzzled him now. Not because his recollections were vague, but because their exactitude had a distant finality.

— I do not recall the full details, Comrade Colonel. How could I?

After which he said something that seemed to come from another language, possibly lost.

— The cold, Colonel Shepilov. It stays in the brain.

— I was there too, said Shepilov, and waited.

— You were there too.

Gruzdev repeated the words mechanically. The taste of tobacco had turned acid on his lips. He had breakfasted too hurriedly, standing up, with the man in the epaulets watching.

— Why was I so obstinate? It is strange, to be sure. I remember how they brought in the dentist.

— Käte Heusemann.

— Yes. Heusemann. And she said I was mad. That I knew

nothing about dental fittings. But that was the point. If a man shoots himself in the mouth his dentures will be smashed, or at least damaged. If the angle of trajectory was such as the X-rays showed, and Captain Vassiliki affirmed, then the bridge on the upper jaw and the window crown on the incisor would almost certainly have been broken. The fittings shown to me were intact, with the exception of some crude scratches on the metal clip. It was these scratches that stuck in my mind. They were white at the edges, as if they had been made very recently, by a nail file and in haste. Then there was the right arm. We know from Dr. Morell's files precisely where Hitler's arm was injured in the July 21st explosion, and how the bones set. On the body submitted to my department for autopsy, the right arm was badly charred. The wrist and elbow joint were like powdered ash. So my reconstruction could only be partial. But it seemed to accord too perfectly with the pathology as recorded by Morell. This is difficult to explain. But evidence that is too clear makes one uneasy. The cracks in the metacarpus, the sutures, the chipping of the bone immediately below the shoulder, were too perfectly apparent. Things that mend naturally, or that retain a partial dislocation, are more blurred. There are always markings and local complications which do not fit the case. Only death composes a perfectly coherent image. Again, as with the dental fittings, it seemed possible—did I say more than that?—that the lesions had been recently and deliberately plotted. That we were meant to observe them and be deceived. Forensic medicine is well acquainted with such devices: toxic substances introduced where there has been no actual poisoning, bones broken after the fact to produce false leads, scars incised in dead tissue in order to conceal identity or suggest false identity. One of my first cases, in Kharkov. I was very young then, and did not know that a tattoo has a peculiar yellowness at the edges when it has been made recently, and on a dead man. I was lucky that Trenin was in charge of the case. Wise as an old fox. He taught me everything. I hear him now: "When the facts are too plain,

36

Nikolai Maximovitch, there is something amiss. There's more in heaven and earth, Horatio. The blind can smell dirt before the wind rises."

And seeing Trenin before him, in his olive-drab cashmere shawl, Gruzdev paused, enchanted. Shepilov looked up from the dossier and said nothing.

— What else can I tell you, Comrade Colonel? It is all there in the records of the preliminary inquiry. The dental fittings and certain aspects of the brachial anatomy. Those were the points which misled me. I withdrew my objections entirely during the hearings before the tribunal.

— But today. Speaking freely, Doctor. As a historian. What would you say now?

The man in the brown suit had spoken so softly that Gruzdev bent forward, almost bowing. And the man's voice, though muffled by the handkerchief at the corner of his mouth, seemed to come out of some dim but irrevocable remembrance, out of a distant gallery or mine shaft of hellish pain. Gruzdev almost panicked.

— Today? I do not understand. What is it you gentlemen wish me to say? I am an old man, Comrade Colonel. I have made a complete statement of my errors. Several times.

Then his eyes glimpsed the book, with its familiar red dust jacket, under a sheaf of papers on Shepilov's desk. He could scarcely contain his relief.

— Academician Ryder's book. I see you have it on your desk, Comrade Colonel. A most remarkable work. The English bloodhound. A veritable Sherlock Holmes. Its account of Hitler's last days is conclusive. Had I known at the time of Academician Ryder's analysis, I would not have been so foolish.

The voice bore in on Gruzdev, nearly inaudible.

— Ryder and British Intelligence are of no concern to us. You will answer my question. Thinking back on all the evidence, do you regard it as possible that you were right? That the body

37

shown to you by Captain Vassiliki's detail was not that of Adolf Hitler?

You will answer my question. Gruzdev knew now where he had heard the voice. In what blinding room and nightmare. But he kept his eyes on Shepilov and breathed noisily.

— Possible?

Gruzdev moved his arms as he had seen actors do in *The Reviser.* If he did not find that gesture out of Gogol he would suffocate.

— That Academician Ryder is wrong? That all the proofs obtained from Linge, Rattenhuber, Hans Baur are false? I appeal to you, Comrade Colonel. Possible? How is a man to answer?

Shepilov loosened a typewritten page from a large bundle.

— Nikolai Maximovitch, you say here that there is a hypothesis to account for the fresh scratches on the dentures, for the clean fractures in the third phalange.

— A double. That the body so clumsily burnt and then left for us to find was that of a double. That the man's bones had been broken just before they shot him in the mouth, and a set of dentures made and carefully preserved.

Gruzdev spoke the words in a monotone, remembering the last time he had dared say them, under Major Berkoff's lashing fist. He was feeling faint. The taste of his own blood seemed in his throat.

The man in brown had risen.

— That hypothesis, Doctor. What is your judgment of it now? Do you regard it as probable?

Gruzdev closed his eyes and asked for a glass of water. He smelled the rank sweat under his arms and between his fingers. It offended him.

— I do not know. I will say whatever you wish me to say. Possible, gentlemen? Everything is possible. *Everything.* I am an old man. *Credo quia absurdum.* Do not torment me. Academician Ryder

Then he stopped speaking, and Colonel Shepilov of the Historical Section motioned him to the door. But they held him there for a moment to tell him that the matter under discussion was not to be referred to in any way. That it was a state secret and that any indiscretion, however slight, would be dealt with as a criminal act.

Gruzdev crossed the bridge and entered the park. He sat on a bench breathing hard but not getting enough air. The light was colder now and he shivered. So it had all been for nothing, the hours in the cellar and the eight years in the camp. He had been right from the start. But why had they called him in now?

A child's rubber ball came bounding toward Gruzdev. Before his eyes it twisted into an insane mask, spitting out yellow, scarlet and silver words. Words that tore the skin off his sweating body. Grusdev covered his face and gave a cry. The child stared at the old man and whimpered, afraid to pick up the ball. Two women turned sharply on a neighboring bench.

Gruzdev got up and walked away. Hitler was alive. They knew it now. And they wanted him, Nikolai Maximovitch Gruzdev, to tell them it was not so. *Ergo est*. Because he is. Because he is they ripped out my nails, and sent me to the ice forest. Because he is I carry in me the memories of the living dead.

Standing on the gravel path Gruzdev laughed aloud and shook with fear.

— Hitler is alive.

He bent low, saying the words to a sparrow, which stood, its pale eyes glittering a few inches from his foot. And repeated them in a wild whisper until the bird moved away.

5

A drawing from his biology textbook, committed to memory in the year in which he left school in a Boy Scout mania for vengeance, crystallized in Isaac Amsel's brain. It pressed on the far edges of his consciousness, barring the wild jabs of panic, the thought, which seemed alive in every bone and fiber, that he would let go at the next step and pitch headfirst into the swamp. It was a histological plate, a vertical cut of an inch of human skin. Through the adipose tissue branched the lacework of capillaries. The white mist of lymph lay in the follicles. And spread among the sinuous roots of hair which, through multitudinous apertures, broke the membrane to form, a fraction of an inch outside ourselves yet inseparably ours, a soft myriad-branched layer. Far beneath, in an interior of hexagonal cells, the candelabrum of veins arched back to its stem and entered the red mouth of the artery.

His own skin must be like that. The exact square inches of it on his left shoulder under the pole of the hammock. But suffocating with sweat, the pores so strangled that the beads of acrid moisture were stiffening into venomous thorns. The raking weight of the pole had flattened the down, pressing each minute hair back into his broken, blistered hide. He imagined the beehive of cells rent out of shape, the blood seeping through its sluice gates and the whole landscape of that torn piece of himself bright with the nameless color of pain.

He would concentrate on that image for the next five steps. Empty his sweating bent skull of every other awareness. He would fill his breath with the remembered smell, linoleum and cool, of the paper in the biology text. He would stop his ears with what his teacher had called the "whisper of lymph" and keep out the sickening sough of water in his boots. Five steps. Then he would void his lungs of the heat and stench and cry out

— I can't go on. I can't. Take the litter. Before I let go. Not another step. Take the pain from me and the heat and needles under my eyelids. I don't care that we've found him. That we must carry him out alive. I can't go on. Not a yard. I will count to ten and get my left foot to touch that floating branch. Then open my hand and let the fire slip from my shoulder. I want to die. *Shema*. Here. *Elohim*. To stretch out till the burning stops.

Isaac Amsel slid his leg forward, pressing his numb fingers to the pole. He knew that he must not commit his full weight until Asher and Benasseraf, the two front bearers, had gained secure footing. They were still in motion; he could see Asher's back trembling, trying to steady, his neck askew like that of a puppet toward the heavy pack which trailed from his right shoulder. Elie was beginning to step forward on the other side of the hammock. The economy of effort in that thin body, the tautness in reserve, had startled the boy on their first marches through the jungle.

The pole dragged along his raw skin and he followed. Toward the sodden branch.

There was a foot and a half of water intervening. Minute darts skimmed across its steaming surface. Dead leaves, matted berries stung open to their gray pulp drew the putrid wash into

41

momentary solidity, but then the bubbles rose catching the dim light, and the fronds of moss drifted apart. Inches above the muck the smell hung visible. Dragonflies and cuara insects hummed through it, their high stilts scarcely brushing the scum. Over the dead leeches gnats swarmed in a rage.

Bending forward to place his boot, the boy saw a sudden clearing of the water. An insect shrilled upward and brushed his mouth. A shape was gliding out of the green fog. Rising toward his leg with a blurred flash of silver.

Isaac Amsel cried out. His cry seemed lost in the lash of water and vine as the four men stumbled.

Simeon spun around. He saw the litter tilt above the boy's frozen face and Asher lurch sideways under the shifting weight. The poncho loosened into the wings of a large bat. With his free hand Elie Barach reached for the half-submerged branch. Feeling the hammock drag away from him, Benasseraf had gripped the pole with both palms. Now his wrists were turning and the carbine, whose strap had slid to his elbow, was slapping against his thigh. Hitler fell out of the blanket.

The swamp was not deep at this point. But crumbling sideways, his right arm pinned to his body, the old man went under. Asher lunged at the tuft of gray hair and pulled him up. He surfaced, shedding water and the sticky filaments of the bog from his eyes and the spare growth above his upper lip. Blinking into the light he shook like a wet mole.

Asher loosened his grip and Elie Barach began laughing. Under his breath but then louder. Benasseraf laughed, shaking water from the hammock. Then Asher. The boy watched, outraged. They were laughing with *him* in their midst, his lips moving strangely. Then the boy laughed also. It seemed easier.

Hitler's arm shot out stiffly, his finger pointing. A braid of silver circled the branch and swayed, weaving and breaking its own image in the dead water. Its mauve hood opened and closed with a pulsing motion. Seeing the man's finger dart at it, the snake stood unmoving. A moment later the thread unwound and vanished with a single flick into the green depths.

Isaac Amsel threw his head back and laughed again. This time at the top of his lungs.

6

Ajalon to Nimrud. Message received. Can you hear me? Ajalon to Nimrud. Glory to God. In the highest. And for ever. The sun stood still over Ajalon so that we could prevail. But then the night stood still. For twelve years. Darkness unmoving. Over us and our children. Can you hear me? Over. But now there is light again, at Gilead and in Hebron, and to the ends of the earth. I tell you there is light as never before. And tonight the stars will dance over Arad. And the world stand still to draw breath, and the dew be like cymbals in the grass. Because he is ours. Because he is in the hands of the living. In your hands. Ajalon to Nimrud. Listen to me. You must not let him speak, or only few words. To say his needs, to say that which will keep him alive. But no more. Gag him if necessary, or stop your ears as did the sailor. If he is allowed speech he will trick you and escape. Or find easy death. His tongue is like no other. It is the tongue of the basilisk, a-hundred-forked and quick as flame. As it is written in the learned Nathaniel of Mainz: there shall come upon the earth in the time of night a man surpassing eloquent.

All that is God's, hallowed be His name, must have its counter-part, its backside of evil and negation. So it is with the Word, with the gift of speech that is the glory of man and distinguishes him everlastingly from the silence or animal noises of creation. When He made the Word, God made possible also its contrary. Silence is not the contrary of the Word but its guardian. No, He created on the night side of language a speech for hell. Whose words mean hatred and vomit of life. Few men can learn that speech or speak it for long. It burns their mouths. It draws them into death. But there shall come a man whose mouth shall be as a furnace and whose tongue as a sword laying waste. He will know the grammar of hell and teach it to others. He will know the sounds of madness and loathing and make them seem music. Where God said, let there be, he will unsay. And there is *one* word—so taught the blessed Rabbi Menasseh of Leyden—*one* word amid the million sounds that make the secret sum of all language, which if spoken in hatred, may end creation, as there was one that brought creation into being. Ajalon to Nimrud. Are you getting me? Perhaps *he* knows that word, he who very nearly did us to death, who deafened God so that the covenant seemed broken and our children given to ash. Do not let him speak freely. You will hear the crack of age in his voice. He is old. Old as the loathing which dogs us since Abraham. Let him speak to you and you will think of him as a man. With sores on his skin and need in his bowels, sweating and hungering like yourselves, short of sleep. If he asks for water fill the cup. If he asked twice he would no longer be a stranger. Give him fresh linen before he needs it. Those who speak to us of their dirt and the itch in the groin are no longer enemies. Do not listen to his sleep. Over. If you think of him as a man, sodden when the rains come, shaking to the bone when you reach the Cordilla, you will grow uncer-tain. You will not forget. Oh I know you will never forget. Rememberers for Jacob. But the memory will turn alien and cold. A man's smell can break the heart. You will be so close now, so terribly close. You will think him a man and no longer

45

believe what he did. That he almost drove us from the face of the earth. That his words tore up our lives by the root. Listen to me. Ajalon calling. Can you hear me? This is an order. Gag him if you must. Words are warmer than fresh bread; share them with him and your hate will grow to a burden. Do not look too much at him. He wears a human mask. Let him sit apart and move at the end of a long rope. Do not stare at his nakedness lest it be like yours. Over to you. Are you receiving me, Simeon? I am not mad. There are thousands of miles to go before he is safely in Jerusalem. You will come to know him as you do your own stench. Look away from his eyes. They say that his eyes have a strange light. Do not leave the boy alone with him. The boy knows but does not remember, not in his own flesh. What this man did. Ajalon calling. Come in, Nimrud. Tell me that you remember. The garden in Salonika, where Mordechai Zathsmar, the cantor's youngest child, ate excrement; the Hoofstraat in Arnhem where they took Leah Burstein and made her watch while her father; the two lime trees where the road to Montrouge turns south, 8th November 1942, on which they hung the meathooks; the pantry on the third floor, Nowy Swiat xi, where Jakov Kaplan, author of the *History of Algebraic Thought in Eastern Europe 1280–1655,* had to dance over the body of; in White Springs, Ohio, Rahel Nadelmann who wakes each night, sweat in her mouth because thirty-one years earlier in the Mauerallee in Hanover three louts drifting home from an SS recruitment spree had tied her legs and with a truncheon; the latrine in the police station in Wörgel which Doktor Ruth Levin and her niece had to clean with their hair; the fire raid on Engstaad and the Jakobsons made to kneel outside the shelter until the incendiaries; Sternowitz caught in the woods near Sibor talking to Ludmilla, an Aryan woman, and filled with water and a piano wire wound tight around his; Branka seeing them burn the dolls near the ramp and when she sought to hide hers being taken to the fire and; Elias Kornfeld, Sarah Ellbogen, Robert Heimann in front of the biology class, Neuwald Gymnasium lower Saxony, stripped to the waist, mouths wide open so that Professor Horst Küntzer could demonstrate to his pupils the obvious racial, an hour of school which Heimann remembered when at Matthausen naked again; Lilian Gourevitch given two work passes, yellow-colored, serial numbers BJ7732781 and 2, for her three children in Tver Street and ordered to choose which of the children was to go on the next transport; the marsh six kilometers from Noverra where the dogs found Aldo Mattei and his family in hiding, only a week before the Waffen-SS retreated northward, thus completing the register of fugitives; five Jews, one Gypsy, one hydrocephalic, drawn up at the *prefettura* in Rovigo; the last Purim in Vilna and the man who played Haman cutting his throat, remember him, Moritz the caretaker whose beard they had torn out almost hair by hair, pasting on a false beard and after the play taking the razor in the boiler room; Dorfmann, George Benjamin Dorfmann, collector of prints of the late seventeenth century, doctor and player on the viola, lying, no kneeling, no squatting in the punishment cell at Buchenwald, six feet by four and one-half, the concrete cracked with ice, watching the pus break from his torn nails and whispering the catalogue numbers of the Hobbemas in the Albertina, so far as he could remember them in the raw pain of his shaven skull, until the guard took a whip; Ann Casanova, 21 rue du Chapon, Liège, called to the door, asking the two men to wait outside so that her mother would not know and the old woman falling on to the bonnet of the starting car, from the fourth-floor window, her dentures scattered in the road; Hannah, the silken-haired bitch dying of hunger in the locked apartment after the Küllmans had been taken, sinking her teeth into the master's house shoes, custom-made to the measure of his handsome foot by Samuel Rossbach, Hagadio, who in the shoe factory at Treblinka was caught splitting leather, sabotage, and made to crawl alive into the quicklime while at the edge Reuben Cohen, aged eleven, had to proclaim "so shall all saboteurs and subverters of the united front," Hagadio, Hagadio, until the neighbors, Ebert and

47

Ilse Schmidt, today Ebert Schmidt City Engineer, broke down the door, found the dog almost dead, dropped it in the garbage pit and rifled Küllman's closets, his wife's dressing table, the children's attic with its rocking horse, jack-in-the-box and chemistry set, while on the railway siding near Dornbach, Hagadio, the child, thrown from the train by its parents, with money sewn to its jacket and a note begging for water and help was found by two men coming home from seeding and laid on the tracks, a hundred yards from the north switch, gagged, feet tied, till the next train, which it heard a long way off in the still of the summer evening, the two men watching and eating and then voiding their bowels, Hagadio, the Küllmans knowing that the smell of gas was the smell of gas but thinking the child safe, which, as the thundering air blew nearer spoke into its gag, twice, the name of the silken-haired bitch Hannah, and then could not close its eyes against the rushing shadow; at Maidanek ten thousand a day; I am not mad, Ajalon calling, can you hear me; unimaginable because innumerable: in one corner of Treblinka seven hundred thousand bodies, I will count them now, Aaron, Aaronowitch, Aaronson, Abilech, Abraham, I will count seven hundred thousand names and you must listen, and watch Asher, I do not know him as well as I do you, Simeon, and Eli Barach and the boy, I will say Kaddish to the end of time and when time ceases shall not have reached the millionth name; at Belzec three hundred thousand, Friedberg, Friedman, Friedmann, Friedstein, the names gone in fire and gas, ash in the wind at Chelmno, the long black wind at Chelmno, Israel Meyer, Ida Meyer, the four children in the pit at Sobivor; four hundred and eleven thousand three hundred and eighty-one in section three at Belsen, the one being Salomon Rheinfeld who left on his desk in Mainz the uncorrected proofs of the grammar of Hittite which Egon Schleicher, his assistant newly promoted Ordinarius, claimed for his own but cannot complete, the one being Belin the tanner whose face they sprinkled with acid from the vat and who was dragged through the streets of Kershon behind a dung cart but sang, the one being Georges Walter who when they called him from supper in the rue Marot, from the *blanquette de veau* finely seasoned, could not understand and spoke to his family of an administrative error and refused to pack more than one shirt and asked still why why through his smashed teeth when the shower doors closed and the whisper started in the ceiling, the one being David Pollachek whose fingers they broke in the quarry at Leutach when they heard that he had been first violin and who in the loud burning of each blow could think only of the elder bush in his yard at Slanič, each leaf of which he had tried to touch once more on the last evening in his house after the summons came, the one not being Nathaniel Steiner who was taken to America in time but goes maimed nevertheless for not having been at the roll call, the one being all because unnumbered hence unrememberable, because buried alive at Grodne, because hung by the feet at Bialistok like Nathansohn, nine hours fourteen minutes under the whip (timed by *Wachtmeister* Ottmar Prantl now hotelier in Steyerbrück), the blood, Prantl, reporting, splashing out of his hair and mouth like new wine; two million at, unspeakable because beyond imagining, two million suffocated at, outside Cracow of the gracious towers, the signpost on the airport road pointing to it still, Oszwiecin in sight of the low hills, because we can imagine the cry of one, the hunger of two, the burning of ten, but past a hundred there is no clear imagining, he understood that, take a million and belief will not follow nor the mind contain, and if each and every one of us, Ajalon calling, were to rise before morning and speak out ten names that day, ten from the ninety-six thousand graven on the wall in Prague, ten from the thirty-one thousand in the crypt at Rome, ten from those at Matthausen Drancy Birkenau Buchenwald Theresienstadt or Babi-Yar, ten out of six million, we should never finish the task, not if we spoke the night through, not till the close of time, nor bring back a single breath, not that of Isaac Löwy, Berlin, Isaac Löwy, Danzig (with the birthmark on his left shoulder), Isaac Löwy,

Zagreb, Isaac Löwy, Vilna, the baker who cried of yeast when the door closed, Isaac Löwy, Toulouse, almost safe, the visa almost granted, I am not mad but the Kaddish which is like a shadow of lilac after the dust of the day is withered now, empty of remembrance, he has made ash of prayer, AND UNTIL EACH NAME is recalled and spoken again, EACH, the names of the nameless in the orphans' house at Szeged, the name of the mute in the sewer at Katowic, the names of the unborn in the women ripped at Matthausen, the name of the girl with the yellow star seen hammering on the door of the shelter at Hamburg and of whom there is no record but a brown shadow burnt into the pavement, until each name is remembered and spoken to the LAST SYLLABLE, man will have no peace on earth, do you hear me Simeon, no place, no liberation from hatred, not until every name, for when spoken each after the other, with not a single letter omitted, do you hear me, the syllables will make up the hidden name of GOD.

He did it.

The man next to you now. Whose thirst and sour breath are exactly like yours.

Oh they helped. Nearly all of them. Who would not give visas and put barbed wire on their borders. Who threw stones through the window and spat. Who when six hundred escaped from Treblinka hunted down and killed all but thirty-nine—Polish farmers, irregulars, partisans, charcoal burners in the forest— saying Jews belong in Treblinka. He could not have done it alone. I know that. Not without the helpers and the indifferent, not without the hooligans who laughed and the soft men who took over the shops and moved into the houses. Not without those who said in Belgravia and Marly, in Stresa and in Shaker Heights that the news was exaggerated, that the Jews were whining again and peddling horrors. Not without D. initialing a memo to B-W. at Printing House Square: *no more atrocity stories. Probably overplayed.* Or Foggy Bottom offering seventy-five visas above the quota when one hundred thousand children could have been saved. Not alone.

But it was he who made real the old dream of murder.. Everyman's itch to clear his throat of us. Because we have lasted too long. Because we foisted Christ on them. Because we smell other.

It was he who turned the dream into day. Read what he said to his familiars, what he spoke in his dancing hours. He never alludes to the barracks or the gas, to the lime pits or the whipping blocks. Never. As if the will to murder and the knowledge were so deep inside him, so much the core of his being that he had no more need to point to them. Our ruin was the air he moved in. We do not stop to count our breaths.

It was he. With his scourge of speech and divining rod. His wrist breaking each time he passed over other men's weakness. With his nose for the bestial and the boredom in men's bones. His words made the venom spill. Over to you, Simeon. Can you hear me?

Do you remember the photograph in the archive in Humboldtstrasse? Munich, August 1914, the crowd listening to the declaration of war. The faces surging around the plinth. Among them, partially obscured by a waving arm, but, unmistakable, his. The eyes upturned, shining. Within twenty-four months nearly every man in the photograph was dead. Had a shell found him out, a bullet, a grenade splinter, one of millions, the night would not have stood still over us. We would have grown old in our houses, there would be children to know our graves.

It was he. The sweating carcass by your side. The man picking his nose as you listen to me or dropping his trousers.

None of the others could have done it. Not the fat bully or the adder. He took garbage and made it into wolves. Where his words fell, lives petty or broken grew tall as hate. He.

Do not listen to him now. Guard him better than eyesight. We must have him alive. Knit the skin to his bones. Carry him if you must. Let him lie in the sun and in dry places. Force his mouth open if he won't eat. Search his teeth for poison and smear ointment on his boils. Tend him more dearly than if he were the last child of Jacob.

Skirt Orosso if you can. The ground is not sure. And keep from men's sight. If it were known that we had him they would snatch him from us. And mock us again.

I shall wait for you in San Cristóbal. Send me news of your position. Each day at the agreed hour. I shall leave here in good time. Life is new in me now. I shall wait for you at the edge of the forest. Ajalon calling. Come in Nimrud. Come in. Can you hear me?

Simeon, answer me. Over to you. Over. This is Lieber calling
this is Lieber
this is

Trapped, the black tick had stung Simeon's ear. The lobe had swollen. Now a warm cotton hum lay between him and the world.

His attention, moreover, strained to interpret the new rhythms of the march. For months there had been at his back, grown familiar to him as the wince of his own muscles, a four-stress motion. By ear, by the antennae sharper than hearing which seemed to pulse from the nape of his neck, Simeon had learned to register the forward progress, the falterings, of Elie Barach, John Asher, the boy, and Gideon Benasseraf, who usually held the rear. After bending a liana he could distinguish, without having to turn around, the fourfold interval during which each man bent the vine in turn for the next to grasp until Gideon let it lash away behind him into the thorny weave of the forest. In the sucking stench of the bog he had been able to mark the position of his four companions as sharply as if he had eyes in his spine.

Now the beat had totally altered.

His thin arms tugging at their shoulders, the right hand jabbing in a constant palsy, Hitler, after his fall from the hammock, had been half-carried and half-drawn through the steaming water by Asher and Benasseraf. At moments Hitler's head brushed against Gideon's cheek like a clump of wet leaves. Where footing was steadier—snake grass plaited to spongy mats, vines cut and wound to a spiral around submerged branches, humps of packed mud iridescent with the sheen of sulfur formed brief shoals and dikes even in the heart of the swamp—Hitler's grip loosened and he came forward on his own.

But whether borne, dragged or laboring at his own pace, the old man had broken the habitual pattern of heavy breathing and snapped branch which Simeon had come to locate in the wake of his every motion. Nearly at each step he wanted to turn around to make out the meaning of unfamiliar shufflings and sudden leaps of water. His back prickled with the sense of a new presence. Behind the slither and frequent pauses in Hitler's progress he could not locate the lighter gait of Isaac Amsel. Who now came last and had added a part of Benasseraf's gear, and the carbine, to his own pack. Yet Simeon knew he must not turn his head.

The yards ahead, more often it was a matter of a few feet, exacted his total attention. He could hardly think of reality any more except as dark green. To exist was to guard one's sweating mouth and hands against an unbroken rush of spiked and thrashing shapes, against blotting creepers that left filaments and small burning shards in one's skin and hair. To Simeon breathing had become a smell musky and heavy as dead water. Unknowing, he had grown new feelers. The scent of rot had only to thicken a little, to steam more densely from the moss, for Simeon to know that rain was near and from which quarter in the green cage of the world it would hammer down. A leathery slide in the barbed grass, an abrupt whorl of stillness in the saw of the swamp cicadas, and he would keep his foot poised waiting for the adder to whip away. A dimpled swelling of the bark told Simeon of the tree scorpion. He could hear the woodpecker in the unseen thicket. That there might be another order of life, where one step followed unheeding on the other, where breath passed cool through open lips, seemed knowledge as distant, as irrelevant to his present being as was Simeon's remembrance—was it still within his reach?—of the last Sabbath of peace in Lemberg, when the end of summer air lay blue around the candles and the grain of cinnamon shone on the white cloth.

The new, often alarming shapes of sound at his back, the lure of Hitler's feet ten yards behind him and the utter watchfulness demanded of him by the swamp, made Simeon insensible to the wisps of noise from the transmitter. He carried the thing with him still, gutted as it was, its delicate skein of wires disheveled. If the damp had not eaten through the canvas wrappings, there were spare coils and circuit boards waiting at Jiaro. Now it was only a weight, a hot rub across his left shoulder and a frequent jab in the small of his back.

Nevertheless, some part of his brain, inexplicably idling or numb to the pressure of the swamp, *had* registered the bursts of static. He understood that the set was alive and picking up a signal though it could no longer amplify or sort it out. When they had taken a break after the collapse of the hammock to let Hitler wring the water out of his trousers, Simeon had swung the receiver nearer to his good ear and listened.

The fret and whine had come through in staccato fusillades. Simeon remembered the double rasp of shotguns in the arcade in October, when he was a small boy. He strained to hear. And imagined Lieber's voice saying urgent words, giving precise indications of help, instructing the party of the planes under way, of the supply drops being marshaled on the edge of the swamp. But instead of being in a frenzy over the failure of the set, over the betrayal of rubber and metal which cut him off from Lieber's guiding genius and assurance of relief, Simeon found himself drifting. The needling at his ear was not being produced by Emmanuel Lieber. The rhythm was wrong. It was not Lieber speaking at the other end of the transmitter, or if these pricks of

55

sound were indeed Lieber's they had been emitted a long time ago. They were reaching Simeon like light waves from a burnt-out star. Lieber was dead. Or had given them up for lost. He had left the airless room in Lavra Street locked, gathering dirt. The mice were at the maps and a large fly lay dead on the silicone mouthpiece. There would be no one at San Cristóbal, no sulfa tablets at Jiaro. Lieber had not been there to receive his call. Who was trying to reach him now?

The thought must have shown. Asher had stopped laughing and was staring at him across the dripping poncho. Simeon pulled himself up, swung the transmitter back over his shoulder and stopped listening.

Or almost. Now, in sight of the day's goal, he could still make out below the shrilling of the bugs the obstinate pulse of static. Simeon let the strap slide down his arm as he lurched the last few yards toward the sandspit.

He had marked the place on the way in but was too preoccupied to cerebrate the precision of his bearings. Here the basket weave of water and shifting ooze had widened to a large pool. Though the drag of swamp continued in the deeps and everywhere around, the water in the pool had a clear black stillness. Forming an almost regular circle it mirrored a round patch of sky unbroken by the sway of vines and the close knit of treetops. The high sun skimmed over the pool like a gold sovereign. Though the winds did not reach them, the waters reflected, in a strange fixity, the tearing of rain clouds and the green and copper of dawn as it streamed across the Cordillera. On one side the pool was rimmed by a crescent of fine sand. From it a spit of ground extended a few hundred yards into the dark funnel of water. Neither the salt stench of strangled vegetation nor the vapor of insects intruded on this small peninsula. Simeon had seen only one sign of life when they passed the sandspit on the march in, a tree toad no larger than the flat of his hand, its horns and the sharp ridge of its spine glinting like pale silver.

Though he had been in the rear, Isaac Amsel splashed past

Simeon at a run and was the first to dump his pack and blanket roll at the edge of the pool. In the dimming light the figures jostled and appeared to move without aim. Hitler's presence, he stood on the verge of the jungle almost invisible against the soft stuff of leaf and nightfall, had splintered the order of march and the close-hammered drill of encampment.

Asher's question woke Simeon from his trance.

— Shall we tie him up? Not that he'd get very far.

Simeon panicked momentarily. Hitler had vanished. Then he saw him, a few feet inside the undergrowth, urinating. A final streak of daylight had caught the old man's face as he bent forward. It lay like a white moth against the flatness of the leaves.

— Yes. Tie him up.

Elie Barach began laying out the Primus stove. He blew on the wick and brushed the grid with his sleeve. The sounds, coming in their right sequence as they did with each sunset, braced Simeon.

— Tie him securely. Use one of the guy ropes.

— Use a long rope, said Elie,

— tie one end to his leg and the other to one of us or the hammock pole. We can hammer it into the ground. That way he can move a bit and be on his own. I don't suppose he sleeps much. And Nebuchadnezzar shall graze, yea like a tethered goat.

— He won't run away, said Benasseraf,

— I'll guard him. I couldn't sleep. I'll stand watch.

And Isaac Amsel flourished the carbine above his head. He had seen the gesture on a poster advertising an American film of espionage and liberation in São Paulo.

— He wouldn't last the night in that bog. He'd die alone not knowing who he was. In a thousand square miles we're the only ones to know. He needs us.

And Benasseraf unrolled the canvas sheets and staked out the pegs for the lean-to.

When Asher knelt before him and tied the rope to his ankle, Hitler moved his lips. He made a hoarse sound but said nothing. Asher knotted the other end to a peg and drove it into the ground between his and Simeon's bedding. Then he dipped his hands in the water and said to no one in particular

— Cold. The water's really quite cold.

Blackness had fallen from the sky at a single stroke. Meeting the blackness of the pool it formed an opaque pillar. It muted the beat of Benasseraf's mallet and the crinkle of the stove. Simeon had noticed before how the sudden night took sounds with it. Only smells stayed distinct. He inhaled the rust sweetness of the tea even before Elie came out of the shadows to hand him the mug. The boy lit the hurricane lamp but its light seemed to recoil from the pressure of darkness. It was only in the shelter that a stain of red showed against the ground and the taut canvas.

The rope had moved a little when Elie carried a mug of tea into the outer darkness. Now it lay still, coiling away from the faint sheen of light. Isaac Amsel crouched next to Elie and opened the tins of meat and noodles. Simeon could see the points of light on the opener but heard no crack of metal. At that instant, from far in the jungle, the cry of a parakeet came high and piercing. The rope quivered, then slackened again.

— I'll take the food to him, said Benasseraf,

— he'll want more salt than that. He's sweating his bones away.

Each man ate inside his own cone of blackness. The line between earth and black water had vanished. Though there was no motion in the air a soft booming, as from some quarry many marches away, reverberated now and again in the deeps of the pool. Benasseraf came back into the patch of light. He drank avidly. Simeon stopped chewing and listened. Now the transmitter was really mute. He tried to recapture the inflection of Lieber's voice, the exact shade of his skin. He couldn't. The darkness sucked everything from him except the sour odor and chill of his own body. He saw Asher look toward the water and

58

pucker his lips. Asher could whistle like a yellow finch, liquid obbligatos that woke the forest to a chatter. But he kept silent and turned back to the shelter testing the rope with his foot.

— I'll get his plate, said Elie.

The boy felt for the water's edge and rinsed the mugs and spoons. His bowels were churning and he farted. Quickly he rattled the tin plates, but they made hardly any noise. He was breathing fast. The night closed on his eyes and mouth like a blotter. When Elie Barach's shadow cut across the lamp, Amsel couldn't even see his own hands. He put down the canteens and hurried to the bushes sweating. The depths of the pool sounded again, a muffled stroke, long drawn out. It went through him like a cramp.

When he returned to the bivouac, stepping wide over the rope, Isaac Amsel saw that Asher and Simeon had rolled themselves inside their sleeping bags. Next to Simeon, seeming to form an enclosure against the reaching chaos of the jungle, lay his re- volver, the holster strap unfastened, the short-wave transmitter, the zinc box of snake serum and Novocain, and Simeon's large flashlight. The mosquito netting was so near Asher's face that it followed the contour of his nose and cheekbone like a cobweb on the effigy of an armored personage, tensed to spring from repose. An egg-shaped hump of shadow, barely distinguishable from the surrounding dark, told Isaac that Barach was at prayers, wrapped in his shawl, his knees close-pressed under his bowed chin. By the outermost lamp, at the point of the sandspit, a red ember brightened and dipped in abrupt arcs. Benasseraf had lit one of his coarse-leaved cigarillos. The ashes flaked into the pool. The boy went to him and sat down in the sand. He saw the stock of the carbine resting against Benasseraf's knee. Gideon's face was turned away from him staring at the night air which dragged on the water like black felt.

— I can't sleep either. Not with him out there.

Benasseraf didn't answer. He didn't want the boy near him. It was a cliché, part of the scenario Lieber had contrived and whose pages they were now turning probably at the cost of their souls. It was part of every bad novel. There had been a time for bad novels. Paper escarpments of them guarding his unmade bed in the rue de Rennes. The drug of pulp, drowsier than mandragora. Bad novels that packed his brain like sawdust in an art-gallery crate and kept the jagged, twisted objects of his memory from crashing about, from piercing the walls of his skull. It was he who resented Amsel most. Who had tried hardest to get rid of him, first in São Paulo, then at Orosso, where the boy should have stayed to watch over the stores of the botanical expedition. It was Benasseraf who found Isaac's flour-ishes and turns of heroic phrase—confetti out of old war films— most exasperating. Nevertheless, or because of this, the boy would seek him out on the march and when they made camp. He could have entered into Elie's tabernacle, into that complicity of prayer and parable which seemed to advance so fluently even through the jungle. Or learned from Asher how to drink life through a straw, barely cutting the rind of the orange. Instead he came to him in patient blackmail. Setting traps for recognition. Precisely as a banal fiction would have it. The son choosing the father.

— You can't sleep either, can you, Gideon? Is it loaded?

— No. Why should it be?

— You don't think he'll try to escape?

— Where to? The bog is alive almost everywhere around us. If he didn't drown there are the ants. Did you see the mud move back there? Simeon saw it. As if a cloud of red pepper were blowing along the ground. They'd scour his bones.

— If I were he I'd try to escape. No matter what. I'd saw the rope with my teeth. Because he must know what we'll do to him. Or be thinking about it all the time.

It was easier to talk than to say nothing. The words blew away with the ash of the cigar.

— And what will we do to him?

— Ah, said the boy throwing back his head. The night soot was in his hair.

— Ah, that's up to Lieber isn't it? And all the others. They must be running wild with excitement. Getting everything ready. They'll try him in the high court. In the highest. And hang him. After breakfast. That's not what I would do. I've thought about it. I wouldn't do it that way at all. Quiet and clean. You don't feel anything. I've read about it. Just a hammer blow, with the hammer in a rag. I'd do it so that he knew it was being done. Every thousandth of a second. And done many times. Not all at once. Snap and it's all over. So he'd wonder about the next time, that's how I'd do it, and hear himself howl. I'd chain him to a stake on top of a pile of wood. So high that he could see beyond the city. And lay a trail of powder or a wick a hundred miles long, winding through every street and coiling around the square. And light it. He'd see the flame traveling nearer. He'd have to watch it for hours. Closer and closer. Just before it reached the faggots I'd jump in front of the crowd and stamp it out. I'd stamp it out with my own heel. And have them light the fuse all over again, at the far end. Or hang him on a pulley just above a vat of acid. Each day someone would come, there'd be tickets or numbers drawn, and turn the crank so that some bit of him would dip in the acid. One turn if you've lost a wife, two for each child. I'd jam a prop in his mouth so that he couldn't scream. Till his eyes burst. Or set his balls in a carpenter's vise. For a few minutes each day. Until he fainted. Putting a timetable on his wall so that he would know exactly when the next session came. And skin his leg to make the lampshade in his cell. How does a man live with the smell of his own skin outside him? Or have a jar with rats, starved rats behind a grate.

— You've got that out of a book. You're not talking about *him*. You're emptying your own mind. Of garbage.

— No, said Isaac Amsel,

— I'd do all those things. I'd do all those things. And keep

61

him alive. And start all over again. What would you do, Gideon, what would you do?

— I haven't thought about it. I'd let him go.

The boy's images were like the sour breath of the pool.

— I'd let him go wherever he wanted inside Israel. With only the clothing on his back. Every single time he wanted food or water or shelter he'd have to ask for it and say who he was. Everyone would know, of course. But I would make him repeat it each time, very loud. "I am Adolf Hitler. I am Adolf Hitler. I beg bread off you, a cup of water. Give me shelter in your house." I'd make him say it loud.

— What would be the good of that? If that's what you want why not let him die in the jungle? Why not turn him loose?

— Why not? I don't know. Imagine it. He'd die a very old man. Well fed. A fat old tourist in the land of Israel.

Amsel slid his knuckles over the butt of the carbine.

— If you feel that way, Gideon, why are you here? You're not telling me the truth. You want him, just like the rest of us.

— You're stupid. No one wants him like anyone else. Each in his own little way. You because. Because you'll pretend you're making good your father's death. Because you've seen too many movies. Brave boy. Sunset. Father avenged.

He tried to flick the ash far into the water. But it seemed to catch in the net of the dark and fell on his boot.

— How do you want him?

— I don't know. Not now. Not like Lieber and Simeon. I don't think it was that way for me even at the start. To me he isn't Elie's Beast of the Seven Fiery Heads. I never wanted him that way.

The boy leaned back, content. Night talk, closer than he had ever had with Gideon. Whom he worshiped. Who was the strongest of the lot. Stronger even than Simeon, or different. Whom they would never have drawn into that cheap deathtrap at Paranã.

— Not to get even. For what? You wouldn't understand. But

when I hear about vengeance, about his eye for an eye, I want to vomit. There can be no vengeance, no making good. Why should history apologize, just to the Jews? Don't stare at me Amsel as if you knew what I was trying to say. You don't. You think it's a game, ten points to each side. Because we've got Hitler and can tear his nails out and wait for them to grow again the dead will sit up and give themselves a dusting. They won't. Not one of them. Not if you parade him over every grave, over every ashpit, not if you dip him in boiling oil six million times. Do you really believe a man can get even for the murder of his children? For what a six-year-old girl saw before she died, for the fear which was so great that she dirtied herself, that she was driven down to the street in her—

He had been told, years after. By Moritz Levenfisch, who, inexplicably, survived. Who had sniffed him out in Paris and was a liar and *shnorrer*. It might not be true. Or perhaps it was. Benasseraf had locked out memory and come to Lieber empty. He had brought only himself. Why remember now? The three children were not clear in his mind. How old would they be this night? Shlomo had been eight when. What was the color of Rebecca's hair? A burnt brown. Even before the fire. He felt frightened and nauseated. As if his foot had missed two steps on a black staircase. He almost turned on Isaac Amsel.

— own dirt. You think that can be made good? You can't be that much of a fool. It doesn't matter. The rest of us aren't any wiser. There are two kinds of Jews left, the dead and those who are a bit crazy.

This time the ash flicked away but went out long before it reached the surface of the pool.

— That's why I don't want anyone to touch him. To torment him, to hang him would be to pretend that something of what he has done can be made good, that even a millionth of it can be cancelled. If we hang him history will draw a line. Accounts settled. And forget even faster. That's just what they want. They want us to do the job for them and put the whole guilt on him.

Like a great crown. *He*'s the one to blame. Let the Jews hang him high. *He* did it all. They must be the ones who know. We're acquitted now. First they nailed up Christ and now Hitler. God has chosen the Jew. For his hangman. Let them carry the blood. We're in the clear. You don't understand, do you? I'm talking mad talk. The leeches have sucked my brain. At the first town we come to we should leave him. Go to the hotel, put him in an armchair and leave him. Then we should scatter, turning away from each other on the run. Not looking back. Let them try him and do what they will. He's *theirs*!

Gideon thought he had shouted the word. Perhaps he had. In his first drift of sleep Asher felt the rope move momentarily. He had looped it across his waist.

— He's theirs.

Saying it once more he almost touched the boy. Isaac Amsel smiled in the dark.

— Gideon,

He didn't have to hurry now.

— Where will you go? I mean afterward. After we hand him over.

— Afterward? I'll go look for Adolf Hitler.

Isaac tried to choose the right laugh.

— You don't think that's he? You think we've got the wrong man? Are you serious?

He wanted to take the lamp and swing it close to Gideon's face.

— I don't know whether that's Hitler. Have you smelled him? He smelled too much like a man. He's got diarrhea. The scourge of God shouldn't smell that way. The real Hitler is inside the mountain. You haven't ever seen the *Riesengebirge*, like the mouth of an old leopard, white-and-gray teeth curving into the sky. The cold breath of those mountains hits you miles away. Listen to the pool, Amsel, listen.

The muffled booming of the gong passed just below them and drummed away into the unechoing forest.

64

— It's much louder than that in the mountains. That's where he's hiding, in the mouth of the black winds with the Redbeard and his armored men. They were Jew-killers too. You can draw gold out of a Jew's bladder if you squeeze hard enough. I read that, carved on the wall in the prison tower at Schwarzberg. I don't think he'd let himself be caught and done to death, not by a few scarecrows wading through a swamp. When a grenade bursts the sharp bits scatter. This is one of his splinters. Perhaps there are many flying about. The thousand-year *Reich* has hardly begun, count for yourself. I know when Hitler will die. I know the day. When the last Jew is dead. Then he'll shout once more, one last bellow, so loud that the mountains will crack, and he'll smile and fall dead on the stone table. But not until then. To be a Jew is to keep Hitler alive.

They heard Elie Barach's steps scuffing the sand as he went to the shelter, still mantled in his shawl.

— Why do you listen to me? Go to sleep. Check the paraffin and go to sleep.

— I want to go with you. Afterward.

— Where?

— To Paris.

Isaac felt such lightness in himself, piercing through the weight of sleep and the churn of his bowels, that he fluttered his hands before the hurricane lamp, a moth beating against the glass.

— To Paris. Where I'll study to become a film director. Oh I know it takes a long time. You've got to know languages; they make you spend six months in the cutting room just watching. But I'll become a director and write my own scripts. Like Jean Renoir. He's the greatest. I've seen everything he's done. I've seen *The River* five times. You remember when the flute stops sounding and you know that the snake has come? I'm going to make a picture about us, how Lieber's men went into the jungle and found Hitler. *Journey into the Green Hell.* Wide screen. No one has learned how to use a wide screen yet, not really. Antonioni faked it. I think he's really a still photographer. No film sense. I'll show how the Chavas surround us and won't let us go until we leave a hostage. Or until one of us fights against their best warrior using a spear set with piranha teeth. Long panning shot of the fight and the circle of spectators. I think I'll cast you in the part of the fighter. You'll win, of course, but we'll have to show a great scar. At the end we'll be seen staggering out of the jungle, bearded, limping, almost delirious, and a great crowd will surge toward us. I'll use a zooming lens to show a sea of faces, ecstatic, unbelieving. We'll hand Hitler over to the waiting guards. Press helicopters overhead, painted bright yellow, cameras looking at my camera. But I'll never show Hitler's face, not full on. Only from the side or in a shadow. In the last frame there'll be the back of his head and Lieber moving toward him.

— And the two heads will become as one.

— Yes. As one. Do you remember *Umberto D*.? Made years ago. I saw it at a Festival of Old Films. There was an old man in that. I don't remember his name. I want him to play Lieber, if he's still alive.

— And use the back of his head for Hitler?

— Yes. No. I don't know why you say that.

Gideon's voice was almost too near.

— I want that old man to play Lieber. There was a marvelous close-up, the light glinting off the rim of his glasses. I'll never forget that. The camera must have been angled from below.

Benasseraf tapped the ash. His cigar was nearly out.

— Why should I go to Paris?

— Because you said you would. I heard you say it to John, in the train. That it was the only place where you could forgive. No. Not forgive. Not exactly. I don't remember the word. But something like that.

Isaac Amsel rocked gently on his heels. It warmed him and made him feel strangely housed to try and remember. They were old friends now laboring to get things right.

— And during the fever you said

Too many things. He carried the still in his mind, perfectly framed, ready for the long touch of his senses. A table fifty yards from the corner of the Place Fürstenberg, the trefoil silhouette of the street lamps almost touching the red-and-white tablecloth. A little while earlier he had walked past the Librairie des Saint-Pères and seen his monograph newly displayed in the window. G. Benasseraf, *agrégé, Le Silence et le poète,* Éditions de Minuit, the characteristic font, tight and a little forbidding, on the off-white jacket. Now, at the restaurant, he had ordered lunch: *pâté de campagne, brochette de fruits de mer sauce béarnaise* with *pommes pailles,* to be followed by the Boursin with its shade of garlic and a pear, speckled gold and burnt to the touch as was the sunlight of early afternoon. Before him the early edition of *Le Monde* with a *feuilleton* on his book. "*M. Benasseraf, dont la plume vive et érudite . . . cette page admirable de probité et d'intelligence sur Valéry . . . qui quoique de souche étrangère maîtrise la sensibilité française comme ne le font que trop peu de nos critiques en vogue . . . dont la lecture de René Char est témoignage philosophique non moins que poétique . . .*" The cold earth savor of pâté was in his nostrils, the sunlight shivered into small eddies and crystals of red fire as it passed through the glass of Gigondas, the bread was new as morning, the chimes of St.-Étienne were striking half-past one, their dry ivory note still clear behind the splash of the fountain. *Werd ich zum Augenblicke sagen.* This perfect moment outweighing eternity, richer than damnation. And she was sitting across the table from him, waiting for Gideon to take the first bite, her hair smoke-brown as September grass, hooded in the soft dartings and quivering of the sun, her hand laid next to his, the cuff of her blouse closed with a charm, an ancient hammered thing of silver which, only an hour hence, in the sudden dark of their room, he would fumble at and unclasp. Her eyes were on the newspaper article mirroring his name but changing it, as her mouth changed his mouth, as the silent weight of her breasts changed his hand when he held them. In a moment he would bring the bread to his teeth and set the reel in motion again. But so long as his being dwelt on that image, on that convergence of all dreams, the chimes marked one-thirty and the sun danced untiring in the burning of the wine.

It was a glossy post card, tourist bait. Made up of all the miracles and reawakenings of his three years in Paris after his release from the sanatorium in Lündfjord. *Silence and the Poet* was unwritten though tenaciously projected. He had been to that restaurant once, but only to watch a friend eat, a shallow friend. He no longer knew his name. The breasts in his hand had been light, tired after short sleep. There had been no one to transmute him. He had not wanted to give that much of himself lest some ineradicable message in the blood carry over to a child his own memories, lest a child be born and grow up carrying with it his knowledge of pain or the monstrous shapes of fear and the inhuman which filled him. The cuff links were real. He had broken a nail toying with their intricate clasp. Who had worn them? A man or a woman? Gideon was no longer certain.

Yet the snapshot glittered inside him with a weird pressure of life. It arrested in a waking dream the otherness of the world, the illusion of total possibility without which the soul falls to a dusty heap. To sit at that particular table and smell the summer in the wine, to write that book and hear the rustle of paper and fireman's fanfare of literary acclaim—*gloire* has the shape of a fireman's helmet—to lie with such a woman in the sea noises of a Paris afternoon, these were indispensable longings. That post card, sharp in every line, was Gideon's remembrance of the life to come.

He hated its banality, the fact that so many other men had taken the same view. It was a bright chromo, common as tinsel. It belonged to every young man in Paris who had read Balzac, who had seen Sartre pause to wipe his glasses in the rue Jacob.

Hope as cliché, as the uplifted finger of the street photographer. Why did these common wonders possess him? Who had been housed in hell. Why had his fantasies not been ennobled and made immune? Benasseraf loathed the quick sensuality of his daydreams. A piece of cheese and its garlic tang sat more solid in his memory than the long hunger in the forest south of Grodny. When he turned imagination on his wife and the three children the focus was blurred and the light too naked. The montage of his unwritten book and of a woman's hand poised over the tablecloth had a wondrous precision. A man whose child has been burnt alive and who has eaten dung in a sewer should know rarer, more exigent temptations.

— No. Not forgive. Not exactly. I don't remember the word. And during the fever you said.

Amsel was near enough the truth. Not "forgive." He had never said that word to Asher on the journey from São Paulo. He had said "become spurious like a child's tantrum." That was the trap of his life in Paris. His hatred and the memories which made up the substance of his life were being nudged away. One by one the words in his mouth were beginning to drift into the future tense. A man whose child has been burnt alive, whose wife has led another of his children into the gas, should use the future tense sparingly. Only to harry time, to make it ripen into vengeance. In Paris it had ripened into books and garlic cheese and the silver skein of cuff link. That was why Benasseraf decamped and sought out Lieber.

— Back to Paris? Why should I? I'm not going back anywhere. I'm setting up a trading post at Jiaro. Kosher meats and shrunken heads.

Isaac could make out that Gideon had turned to him, that he was speaking to him more directly than ever before. But he knew he was losing him. Gideon cracked stupid jokes whenever his thoughts were distant.

— Look, said Isaac,

— look what I've been hiding. Even Simeon doesn't know.

He had got to his knees and was rummaging furiously in his pack.

— Look, Gideon.

He was on his feet, swaying and coiling like a wisp of smoke. He was clutching something, a small oblong. He gyrated, teasing and triumphant, beating a tattoo in the muffling sand. Suddenly, it was the first glint of light, Benasseraf caught a flash of metal. Still arching to and fro, Isaac Amsel began pulling out a thin, bending stalk.

— Look, Gideon, look. A transistor. A Japanese one. Nakima. I bought it in São Paulo. It picks up short-wave. Sometimes. When the nights are clear.

— Why have you been hiding it?

— Mine, said the boy,

— mine. Not yours, not even Simeon's.

He was laughing, darting out of reach.

— No one would steal it from you. And stop dancing. Why are you dancing? You're a fool, Isaac.

— I bought it with the money Father left me. Before he went. It took nearly all I had.

— What good will it do you? You won't pick up anything. Not out here.

The boy was still laughing and shushing and putting his finger to his lips. He turned the little radio around and around, now above his head, now at arm's length, whipping the antenna through the heavy air.

— Listen. Can't you hear?

His whisper was startling. It carried. Sounds were beginning to lift and take shape. The pool had stopped booming. Somewhere, quite near, a bubble broke and the rings glinted in the water.

The whisper had turned to a burst of static, needles showering a distant forest in the Cordillera. Isaac stood frozen. Only his wrists moved, banking the transistor now to the side, now upward, the antenna tracing delicate loops like a fly rod.

— Listen, Gideon. Can't you hear it now?

And in the same moment in which he looked up, at the break of light, Benasseraf heard it.

— *hombre hombre hombre mío*

Light tided in a sudden bright stain from the center of the pool. The dark spilled along the edge of the jungle. Gideon was on his feet watching the canvas flap, the banana trees and the bodies of the sleeping men surface, their black forms edged with a silver contour. In the light of the sudden moon the air cleared and sounds quickened. A sand crab scuttled past his foot leaving a braided spoor.

— I've got something. Listen.

From one of the senders on the vast perimeter of the Amazon Basin.

— *hombre hombre hombre mío*

A woman singing, and behind her the oily slide of the tango. Late-night music. Incessant, always the same and inescapable up and down the entire continent, from Guyana to the Cape. Greasy as the *cantina* floor.

— Now you can hear it.

From San Martín. Or Orosso. No, there was no station in Orosso, only the wireless in the shack by the airstrip. But the new radio tower at Vila Branca might reach. It seemed almost impossible. Across the desolation of the grasslands, the web of the falls, the Cordillera, the muffling rag of the swamp.

— *bésame bésame hombre mío*

The boy stood rigid, the transistor away from his body. His eyes were on Gideon's; they had gathered the new light and were dancing.

— *míííooooo*

Her trill lifted and flexed like a monkey's tail before vanishing in the hot thump of the saxophone. Then, at once, the voice started again.

— *salida del sol salida d'amor*

The rope was moving.

Asher jerked up out of his first sleep feeling it slide across his wrist. Simeon lifted his head. In the moonlight the hurricane lamps had dimmed to a candle flame. The rope was moving on the sand.

— *flores de mi corazón flores*.

The voice reached them. Asher remembered the butter gone rancid on the march to Jiaro. Simeon sat up. A slow shadow passed across the tent cloth. Benasseraf saw him, his face like a plaster mask, the hair glued to it. He was shuffling toward Amsel, his hand cupped to his ear. The top button on his fly was undone.

— Music. Music, said Hitler.

The boy turned and sprang back. He swung the radio away from Hitler in a wild toss. It dangled from his wrist and the strap twisted.

— Let me hear the music. I haven't heard music. Oh in a long time. Many years perhaps. *Blumen*. It is a long time since I have heard a woman sing.

— No. No.

Amsel was yelling. Yelling so the forest rang.

— No!

Hitler stood, staring at him.

— I won't harm the radio. I want to hear the music. Only the music.

The box had gone silent but the minute sphere at the tip of the antenna continued to vibrate.

— Stop shouting, said Benasseraf,

— stop it.

He was shivering and threw his cold cigar into the pool.

72

— *flores de mi corazón flores*.

— Shit

Rodríguez Kulken, coming to and shaking off the sour netting of his sleep, said it to himself. Then again

— Shit

under his breath, spitting it languidly at the back of the neck of the woman who lay beside him snoring. He hated the song. He hated the singer, Carmelita Rosa, whose treacle voice choked his earphones nightly as he cut across the sender from Brasilia. He hated that song because the syrup of its tune, tum tum ta ta tum ta, stuck to his brain. As the mango seeds stuck to the roof of his mouth. Now, more awake, Kulken passed his tongue over the stump and cavity on the upper left side. But together with the taste of singed rubber and sleep—the woman's coffee was a foul thing, an outrage here where the upland bean could be had dirt cheap—came the thrum of the song. *Flores* ta ta tum ta tum *mío cor mío cor*. It had been the last thing in his earphones. And had stayed trapped under the net buzzing deep down into his heavy sleep.

Rodríguez Kulken caught the full scent of himself and said
— *Merde*
but no longer in uncertain consciousness. Across the rancid
shoulder of the woman who lay beside him snoring he could see
the milk-gray light of early morning. Kulken kept his front door
ajar and only the screen door closed. The Indians and Ruiz
Manola, who ran the commissary and was *imperador* as far as
his paunch and drugged eyes could reach, told him that he was
loco. To keep his door open at night when the jungle exhaled—
you could hear the first long sough of breath at sundown—and
the poisonous air blew into Orosso. But Indians were shit and
Ruiz Manola a loudmouthed pile of ordure. Kulken knew about
malaria. All you had to do was take plenty of quinine and keep
your bowels open. Fresh air never killed a man. As it was, the
house stank. Scour it, break your nails in the cracks between the
floorboards, the fungus thrives. At night you can hear the damp
crawl, hungrier than termites.

— Orosso is a cesspool in hell. *Una latrina nel inferno. Ein
Scheissloch in der Hölle. Une pissottière en enfer.*

Rodríguez Kulken said the litany each morning. Sometimes
he added responses in Portuguese, in Dutch or in what he knew
of Bororo. He said it before emptying his bladder. To affirm his
erudition, to tune the fine strings of his worldliness and remind
himself, in the scum and bog of his present sojourn, of loftier
stations. He knew the tongues of men and their several nations,
he was a condor among mice. And once more, but this time like
an *aubade* bugled in his own honor, Kulken said
— *Merde*
whereupon he rose and stepped across the sleeping woman
not kicking her. He would do that later, grinding the cork sole of
his sandal into the small of her back. She would wake, extract
the ball of gum from between her teeth and grin to know him
there. Now he wanted to be alone. The tune was still buzzing in
his skull but growing faint. He would be free of the filthy thing
in a moment.

Kulken watched the bronze stream foam into the mottled bowl. By the time it reached Orosso beer was flat. Or Manola had spat in it. And the greasy bitch still snoring under the raised mosquito netting couldn't keep the ice from melting in Kulken's cooler, not if he showed her a dozen times and bloodied her mouth in the bargain. Indians were dung. Whatever Father Girón might say. The ones that looked human were dangerous. They made it hard to tell. Like Teku, the mongrel, who slithered in from Jiaro with soft monkey skins and carved fish bone and had contracts with the Chavas—or so it was said. Kulken shook his member thoughtfully and straightened up, his back tingling with the new emptiness of morning. When he remembered.

He had dreamt of a motorcycle. It had barreled through his sleep just before the song had come back. The rest of the dream was a blur but the tattoo of the engine stayed loud like one of the 500-cc Hondas he had seen lashing around the circuit in Montevideo. Why should Rodríguez K. dream of a motorcycle? he inquired of himself, with solicitude still stroking his foreskin. Of course: his spell as a dispatch rider for ITT in Barcelona just after the war.

Kulken belched and inhaled the acid freshness of the outhouse.

Barcelona in the late spring of '45. Gunning the engine on the dilapidated Harley, the pride of the ITT stable, out of the chill courtyard into the white sun of the Calle Mayor. Up the sugar-loaf and down the hairpins, twisting around the eucalyptus gardens and through a crazy chute to the harbor. Kulken had been *el diablo,* the red spark. No other rider could touch him. He had driven by smell knowing that he must change gear and throw his leather-encased body to the left at the precise instant when the eucalyptus faded and the first whiff of fried oil charged to meet him from the Ramblas.

His legs still apart on the cold dirt floor, Rodríguez Kulken threw back his head. Memory breached the dike.

False papers. Real people carry false papers. Only queers and

Belgians travel under their own names. R. Kulken had been many tints and delicate stipples. He knew how to coax the metal prongs through the stiff paper in a Danish driving license so as not to betray a change of photograph. Or where the gum loosened in a *Livret militaire* (he had carried one in Metz). The filigree of an Irish passport enchanted him and he retained in his left thumb the remembrance of the perforations, so intricate yet easy to counterfeit, of a Moroccan *permis de séjour*. It had almost cost him his balls to get that piece of pasteboard. The stapler with which the Consul General of Ecuador in Antwerp affixed his seal to a visa was locked away in a cabinet—*Compagnie des coffre-forts de Liège 1911*—set between the two east windows in the back room. The lock yielded to a hairpin.

To know this was knowledge. Kulken's brain was packed with sharp-edged monads of exact wisdom. He knew where the night express from Oporto, the 9:14, slowed down before entering Lisbon. He knew that the lack of proper lighting at the south end of the customs shed at Fishguard made it easy for a man to squat in the pools of shadow and wait for the tea break which came at 10:55 after the second ferry. Knowledge. Not the spindrift that fogs the minds of ordinary men. But nuggets, fine as Björnske ball bearings, and gathered at a price. Kulken kept them polished for instant use by a study, more exhaustive than that of the Mayanos runes, of the only real truths that men have set down: timetables, shipping registers, customs regulations, ordinances from the Bureau of Standards, visa applications, questionnaires addressed by the Principality of Liechtenstein to all who would incorporate, triplicate certifications obtainable from the Panamanian office of flag registry, the *Bulletin commercial de la Banque du Niger* invaluable for its schedules, more evocative of the scent of forest and sea than any verse, of soya and coco transfers. Kulken had flicked the gnats out of the maelstrom of his reading lamp and pored over the monthly newsletter of the Agence Havas and the *Zettel für Devisenhandel* of the Düsseldorf Finanzamt. He knew how thirty-day bills were discounted in Trieste and the name of the daughter of the widowed dispatcher at the Bergen marshaling yards. She had a passion for nylons and yellow plastic raincoats.

Mi corazón flores de mi

That was garbage. False as an import license for Honduran teak. The truths of life spoke from ruled paper and columns of incorruptible figures. No man was himself for long, but hollow and veering as a wind sock. The fact—rooted in the taste for peyote of the sheriff of Small Springs, Texas—that the easy ford into Mexico 19.4 miles southeast of Juárez was never patrolled before midnight on the second Wednesday of the months between October and June was a solid beauteous thing. It would not crumble in one's palm. A man could stake his mortal soul on it. Rodríguez Kulken had, twice.

Not that his papers were, in the ordinary sense, false. How could they have been true? Kulken remembered his mother. She owned a green cardigan which enveloped his entire sense of childhood and there had been an almond smell in her hair. He could not sever that smell from the recollection of a gravel path behind the *pension* in Ostend where they had, for reasons unfathomable, moldered during the early 1930s. Who was his father? A Flem, said the chiromancer in the fairground in Cincinnati squinting at the touch of pepper and flax in Kulken's eyebrows. But the barber in the Posthotel in Solothurn had opined, through the steaming caress of the towel, that "Monsieur has a fine mouth, a Semitic mouth." No matter. He had shed his skin whenever necessary. He had left it in station lockers and on coat hangers in empty hotel closets. What had they made of the Homburg, still quite new, he had left deliberately on the top shelf in the King's Arms at Bradford or of the hair dye flushed imperfectly down the toilet in the *entresol* w.c. of the Hotel Astoria in Belgrade? This was the century of the borrowed skin. Men who knew their fathers or had come of age in a single house were freaks. The poplars were down, their roots a dead tangle sticking out of ditches. It was a good time for the long-legged and those who could make a bundle of their shadows. The roads themselves had begun to move under the persuasion of the bombs.

They had almost speared him, at the *Poste Restante* counter in the main post office in Geneva. He had forgot the number of his *casier*. He hesitated a minute and the sirens of the police cars had started up in the rue des Bergues. 832. Kulken hated that number but would never again forget it. He had made the Rosière tramcar on a dead run. Where had he switched to the Nord line and shaken them off?

Kulken narrowed his eyes and sucked in his cheeks in fierce concentration. A fireball exploded only a yard from his stretched skin. He flinched and grabbed for his crotch. A cold shaft passed through his kidneys.

Again the rooster crowed and bright knives spun in the morning air. Kulken gathered up his pajama bottoms and heaved out of the privy. The stinking fowl. Its cry had dried up the past; all the rich shades were receding.

When he wanted to, Kulken could move fast. On the floor of the yard his shadow grew to a thunderous fist. The bird shot its neck to one side and flounced away in a puff of red and dusty orange.

Kulken aimed a high kick. His sandal slapped the wall of the shed. The rooster lifted a leg and Kulken wondered momentarily at the cruel, ancient shape of the thing. His rage ebbed and he turned toward the house feeling the night damp of the clay between his toes.

— *Cojones.*

He breathed the word in a salute to the sun now spilling against the horned spine of the Cordillera and dispersing the haze which drifted across Orosso from the falls. He straddled the woman's jumbled form, saw that the shift had bunched well above her buttocks and lay down.

He had been keeping late hours.

For three weeks he had been listening. Till his eyeballs ached. The leather arc of his headset was black with perspiration and

left a swath in Kulken's thin hair. Monitoring Nimrud and Ajalon. Gleaning through the static and the oily wash of music from
Pernambuco, from Rio or Brasilia, as its loud, ghostly amours
crisscrossed the pampa and the Amazonian forest, a code out of
Revelation, an alphabet reversed and permuted out of Chronicles
and Malachi. He had picked up, his skull hammering, the weave
of names out of Joshua 15

    — *Kirjath-baal which is Kirjath-jearim and Dannah and
Kirjath-sannah which is Debir and Eltolad and Chesil and Hor-
mah*

    (the latter repeated and followed by a signal reading Exodus
30: xxiv)

    — *And of cassia four hundred shekels*

    (as his contact had pointed out the text should read *five* hun-
dred)

    — *after the shekel of the sanctuary and of olive oil an hin*

At which monosyllable Rodríguez Kulken had found himself
staring like a man drugged.

At one point, when the rain swashing against the roof had
made it almost impossible to hear anything clearly, the message
had been some kind of acrostic threading between Numbers 33

    — *and they departed from Kibroth-hattaavah and encamped
at Hazeroth and they departed from Moseroth and pitched in
Bene-jaakan and they removed from Bene-jaakan and en-
camped at Hor-hagidgad*

and Matthew 1, xii–xv. In which latter text the begettings
had been scrambled so that Achim begat Salathiel and Sadoc
found himself to be great-grandfather to Jechonias.

Not that Kulken had to do the deciphering. Let the office in
Montevideo break its balls over *Golan in Bashan with her sub-
urbs,* and London figure out why II Samuel 9: x had been flashed
thrice, on the night after the transmitter had moved three degrees
southeast of Jiaro, but with a change in the canonic number of
servants

    — *Mephibosheth thy master's son shall eat bread never at*

my table. Now Ziba had fifteen sons and twenty-three servants

For the rat's fodder they gave him Kulken was doing enough. More than enough. There were nights when his fingers had swollen to pale grubs just transcribing the stuff, trying to separate the syllables as they crackled or whispered out of the jungle. There had been thorns in his ears; he had felt them bleed.

Kulken had understood. Oh right from the start. Even that turd Manola had understood. Orchid hunter? Not this lot. Not for all their botanical atlases and best-quality butterfly nets and Leyden jars. Hunters for men. Jew-hunters. Manola had known almost as soon as the boy had come into the commissary with his supply list. Fishhooks, nylon line, Zippo windproof lighters (United States Army surplus), Benzedrine, briquettes, quinine, .38-caliber ammunition, sulfa. When the boy and the other man, the thin one with the greasy locks, had asked for a stretcher, with extra carrying poles, Manola, who had none to sell, said

— Those must be heavy orchids you're after, orchids with a backache.

But neither the boy nor the man had laughed.

There had been other botanical forays. They had plucked Eichmann and Stangler. Ottmar Kühnhardt's body had turned up at the municipal dump in Punta Blanca. The man's eyes had been gouged out. Or so it was noised. They had almost trapped Mengele.

But there was bigger game. Kulken knew, even before that pimply nit of a contact in Montevideo had told him. They were after Bormann, still. They wouldn't let go. Not after all the false leads and the killing of their best man in Paraná. Martin Bormann. He was a fish bone in their throats.

So Kulken had been instructed to take leave of absence—recurrent jaundice—from the flea circus in which he was employed, the Stella Maris Travel & Shipping Agency, and had come to Orosso. Which was the world's anus. He had been there, in it up to his eyebrows, for three weeks, monitoring, passing back to Montevideo the weird chatter of Nimrud and what he could bug of distant Ajalon.

He didn't think they'd get him. Not in that patch of hell. Not alive, that is. Perhaps they'd find his jawbone on a Chava bracelet or spoon guava from his polished skull. They were fools. They had bartered the fact for the dream and it had made their breaths rancid. Not that Rodríguez Kulken hated Jews. He had made up his mind about them a long time ago when he had seen them whore and beg for visas in Lisbon. They were the snot of the human race. From time to time every man had to pick his nose and suck his fingers clean. Kulken liked to pick his own nose, particularly after sex, and had perfected a delicate probing. If it hadn't been the Jews it would have been someone else—the Sinhalese, for instance, or half-breed Flemings. Killing Jews was a piece of stupid ingratitude. Like scraping one's nose *too* clean.

So he didn't wish the poor bastards ill as they burrowed into the jungle but only prayed they would hurry and give up their fool's errand.

That cordial wish had soured to a dull rage as he found himself nailed, night after stinking night, to his transmitter, either snatching at the wisps of speech from beyond Jiaro or being plagued by queries and commands from London (that, of course, was where the queer from the *Review of the River Plate* got *his* orders).

Kulken was on the point of spewing up the whole business; he had eaten his fill. He was going to pack up his gear and return to the coast. Signals had been growing fainter and more riddling. Remote Ajalon hardly responded or only in wild bursts. One whole night there had been nothing to monitor except the disc jockeys out of Brasilia. Before his smarting eyes the needle swung through an arc of tangos and static. When suddenly.

In the first hour of morning.

Recumbent now, his hand idling in his crotch, Rodríguez

81

Kulken remembered. He was not a man lightly stirred. But this had made the skin tighten over his temples. A cry out of the forest. White and sharp as a snow-crystal.

— *One thirty-six. One thirty-six. Oh give thanks unto the God of gods.*

As if a near fire sang in his earphones.

— *and slew famous kings; for his mercy endureth for ever.*

No cipher now. Only that cry of triumph lancing the morning air and vibrant in him still.

— *Sun stand thou still upon Gibeon, and thou Moon in the valley of Ajalon.*

The cry was in his marrow, blinding.

— *And there was no day like that before it or after it that the Lord hearkened unto the voice of a man.*

Kulken had strained to catch the answering sound, the ring of pipe and timbrel from the East. He had held his breath till the veins hammered in his neck. Nothing had come. Not another syllable. He had passed the news to Montevideo where the squit would get off his soft ass, preen himself and send the message to London: *Orchidacis muscata amazonia*. And take the credit.

Kulken had been told to keep listening, to chart the movements of the party as it headed back to Jiaro. He'd listened till his spine creaked. *Nada*. As if their sender had failed. He'd slept and listened again. Nothing on the second night. *Flores del mío cor flores*. And slumped under the netting numb with exhaustion.

Kulken closed his puffed lids. A pleasant warmth rose between his thighs. His hand strayed to the woman's buttocks, paddling the brown half-moons and exploring the cleft. Kulken loosened his pajamas and began to turn sideways. Just then his drowsy thoughts missed a step and a sharp jolt went through him. That was no dream of a motorcycle. There had been an engine hacking and whining above the roof. It had awakened him. Motorcycle, hell. A plane had landed in Orosso. Just after sunrise.

The figure bulked in the doorway cutting off the light. Kulken's eyes opened wide. He saw the neatly creased whipcords and the yellow leather of the pilot's boots. American. And this time Rodríguez Kulken said quite loud

Scheisse.

9

When to Rabbi Jehudah Ben Levi, God, hallowed be His
Name, dictated the Torah, greatly against His instincts, for the
Word had been until then living, seed burning in the flesh because unwritten, might there have been an error made? Because
the stylus slipped or the wax of the tablet flaked in the bronze
heat of the Babylonian day. Because a gnat had lodged in Jehudah's ear. Because, for a millionth of a second, the Master had
drowsed. Because God, may He forgive the libel of my thought,
chose to plant one tare in the harvest of His giving, one false
accent, one letter wrong, one word out of place, out of which
speck has grown till it smothers man the black tree of our hurts.
Out of which has sprouted the knife between my toes and the
pus hammering at my heel, out of which rises the acid in my
baked mouth and the red cry of my neck where the pack rubs.
Out of which have swarmed the green flies that hang on the wet
sore in my crotch. The black tree of life whose shadows are like
nets around my feet and sicken the brain. Whose roots rear out
of the swamp to trip me, whose vines will slap my face at the

next step, now, O God, hallowed be Thy Name, I am falling, whose droppings are the slime in my hair and the stench the stench the stench. I have not fallen.

But *which* word? Which letter or vowel sign or number? It may be only one digit in the numbering of the people or of the cubits of terebinth prescribed for the outward pillars of the tabernacle. Which *iod* has been omitted, which *gimel* misplaced in the three million and eleven characters of Torah. Which being thus imperfect has brought to man not peace not love not clean water but the stench the razor under my sole the needles in my shoulders where the strap burns. Not linen to lie in at evening but the rubber sheet stinking in my hand. Not the child's step in the lit house but *his,* just behind me now, at the root where I fell. Almost fell. Praised be Thou that hast led us.

Which word, which word?

The most learned Isaac of Saragossa declared that the error was in Genesis 22: i. God would command an old man to slay his child but not *tempt* him to do so. Temptation is vile, like a memory of blue air and open sea here in the caldron of the swamp. Nathaniel Ben Nathaniel of Gdansk had, in 1709, conjectured that Rabbi Jehudah had misheard, O ugly mystery of misprision, Exodus 15: xx, for though it be right to dance before the eyes of Pharaoh's drowning host it is wrong to *strike timbrels.* That dance must have been a heavy and silent thing like the hover of the honey wasp in the jungle.

I can't go on much farther,

thought Elie,

the sweat blinds me and draws the flies. They cover my mouth.

In Mainz, Ephraim the Cabbalist had taught his disciples that the mistake was to be found in the seventy-eighth letter of the thirty-third verse of the 26th chapter of Numbers, seventy-eight being the cipher of Tammuz the hanged one, thirty-three that of the degree of Mercury when it is in the house of the crab and twenty-six

85

O God let me take twenty-six steps more before I fall and take the knife from under my feet and let cold water.

But Ephraim had been burnt and Gamaliel of Messina, the learned of the learned, had written, in a hand disguised and in a midrash found only after his death, that the Name of God in the Torah, be it sanctified for ever and evermore, was a false name, that even that Name which no man may pronounce was, as compared with the true Name, no more than the dust of dung when set beside rubies. Each time we call upon Him we call in error and cough like toads in the green scum. Lance the boil under my arm whatever be Thy Name. Bring me to firm ground. Simeon is falling. Simeon. And the boy is shouting. The flies are in my breath. My breath is like a stink. My own master, Shelomoh Bartov, said to us that the unfathomable error, the breach through which evil has rushed on man, was the word *and* in Leviticus 10: v. He said it with such sadness that none of us dared question him. We pored over the text in feverish wonder. A word without shadow, a word lighter than a mote in a sunbeam.

Why *that* word? So I asked. Whereupon the Master called me a dunce, one who understands less than a *goy,* and answered, as in a song to himself, why that *and*? For the reason deeper than reason that it could be any other. And had begun to sing louder and driven us out of *cheder,* like mice, before the song would lift him from the ground. Shelomoh Bartov who was a just man and who danced in the fire pit at Grodny.

Where I ought to have been with him. It would have been quicker. Than this red scratch in my neck. Quicker than this march which is like many deaths. Death up to the groin, death where the pus hammers, where the buckle scrapes across the blistered skin. Blasphemy. The flies are on my tongue. If Simeon doesn't call a halt. But *he* is keeping up. I heard his step behind me. Stronger than yesterday. He takes small hops like an old frightened man. He *is* frightened of the swamp and the fright

86

pricks him. Like an old puppet of a man in little hops. The thorns have scratched his cheek. Now I know which word it is. Deuteronomy 2: xxv: and shall *tremble*.

Benasseraf's trembling had not stopped. The shakes began as he turned from the pool that morning, a slow pounding out of some broken, feverish place beneath the skin. It jerked at the corners of his mouth and made the sweat cold between his fingers. Elie Barach had watched Gideon's back as they set out. Under the blackened shirt, under the carbine strap and the lanyard on which he carried two water flasks, Gideon's ribs and backbone quivered. At every few steps a drum roll beat under Gideon's skin from the neck down and the flasks tinkled. Elie could smell the sweat in Gideon's hair. And sourer than sweat the smell of the fever. It made his own heart race. Simeon knew. Elie could tell by the frequent short halts. By Simeon's decision that Asher bring up the rear.

The fever had passed to the forest. The ooze shook under their feet. Daylight vibrated in sharp jabs, out of reach above the dank shivering vines. Benasseraf had his teeth set and walked in a hunch as if carrying through the mist of the bog a fragile, knife-edged burden. Now and again he would bend low and emit a choked cry.

They stopped where a hummock of swamp grass, its thorny blades high as a man, protruded from the morass. Isaac Amsel sat down in the green cage and picked at a bleeding scab. Simeon had his hand on Benasseraf's left shoulder. He felt the tremors pass through his own arm. Their faces were close in the thick air.

— Gideon. *Mensch*.

The electric eel was loose in Gideon. He clenched his teeth against the next jolt.

— Have you taken?

Early that morning Asher had tapped the powder into his unsteady palm.

— You've got to take more. You'll break in pieces. Do you want us to carry *you*? *He* can walk. He's been nimble as a goat. Stop it. You'll break if we go on.

The low cry and Gideon's teeth unlocked.

— I've had worse attacks. I. I. Don't stop. Not here. It's the swamp. It makes the fever

A spasm shot through him. Simeon tightened his grip. He smelled Gideon's sick breath.

— makes the fever worse. I can make it. If we reach dry ground. I.

They swayed and argued, close as wrestlers.

— We're getting you out of here alive. If we have to camp a week.

— Let me be, Simeon. I'm better when I keep going.

He fumbled for the quinine and the chain of the flask tinkled loud.

— I am better. Let me. We have to move.

Gideon tensed his body and swallowed the drug. As he straightened, a cold current passed down his spine. He dropped the water bottle. Simeon bent down and their cheeks brushed.

— We're stopping here until you're better.

— If we stop here I'll. Get us to dry ground. We can't be too far. I'm better already. Not here.

A bird's egg lay in the mud near Asher's foot. He looked closely. It was teeming with red dots, minuscule, devouring swamp lice. He bent lower still. He thought he heard a sound, like the scratch of a nail far off. A smell of sulfur rose at him.

They hacked their way through the dripping net. For the first time Amsel was front man. Simeon had dropped back to be with Benasseraf.

When he swung the machete Isaac pivoted on his hips and forced his shoulders down as Gideon had taught him. His wrists were swollen. When the blade tore through nothing but dead vines or tree moss it wrenched him off his feet. At other strokes it cut clean and the white sap spurted. At every few yards Isaac wiped the edge. Sodden fibers and thorns stuck to his fingers. Once, absently, he touched his muddied knuckles to his mouth and spat violently. Something jellied had moved across his lips. The vegetation arched above his head.

The six men slogged knee deep through the swamp. In the fitful light the water gave off an oily sheen. The cutlass slashed a windless tunnel through the lianas. Rats slid away, their eyes blind and blood-rimmed. Between strokes the boy spoke to himself.

We are in the sewers. They run west-southwest under the ghetto wall and come up in Novy Swiat. But we've missed the right grate. If I lift the cover now there'll be a boot standing on my face.

He hacked faster. Too fast. Wasting motion and slicing too high so that the spikes whipped back and tore their legs. His lungs hurt. There was no touch of life in the air. As if the bog had drawn and exhaled the same dead breath over a million years. The harder he breathed the more he seemed to choke. A rubber mask pressing down.

Isaac Amsel lashed out with his free arm but the leaves lay heavy on his face. He bent double, panting. Behind him Simeon waited. The boy felt a drilling inside his head. The sound rose to a white screech and filled his ears. He swung his head groping for air. The machete dragged him down. He was going to faint. But the sound was too loud. It spiraled above him and behind. It drowned the chattering of Gideon's teeth and the slither of the rats. Hitler was jabbering and pointing upward.

— Like Stukas. Rrrrrrr. Blitzing.

The fever had opened the sores on Gideon's legs. High in the massaranduba tree a brown cluster, lice-ridden and mantled in sleep, had caught the odor of blood. The brown furry grape burst. The bats plummeted, their wings flaring. They found a rent in the canopy of leaves. They careened in the hot shadows shrilling. Their brown leather wings slapped the cane grass and crazy for flight they wheeled from the thrashing men. But the thorn brakes and hollow of vines held them caged. They dived at the hot smell in the trodden grass and screeched.

— Rrrrrrr

said Hitler, ducking. The bat veered away, a strand of gray hair in its crooked thumb. A brown shape tore at Asher's knee. He kicked wildly and for a moment the bat lay on its back, its belly the color of smoke. Then it flew straight up, inches from his face, its screech like a file across his teeth.

— *Die Vampire*

cried Hitler

— the drinkers of blood

and fluttered his hands in front of his face. A bat skimmed Isaac's hair. The sound whipped like wire across his skull. Now the leech came in again. He could see its eyes, green as mold, and the skin pinched around its wet nostrils. Its fox's ears were taut in flight. He stood paralyzed, his throat muscles pounding. The bat was driveling. As it swerved its spittle flecked the boy's cheek. Amsel cried aloud. The air rushed out of him as from a man drowning. He swung the machete in a crazy arc and cried again.

A small bat writhed in the leaves, its wing pinned under Simeon's foot. Its other wing slashed the air. A wild piping came through its teeth. Simeon bent down. He wanted to touch the raging thing, to pass his finger over the quivering stays. The bat watched him, its eyes bursting at the rim. For a second it lay motionless, its claw open. Simeon wondered at the delicate curve of the nails. Hands of a blind child. Then the biter exploded under his foot. The animal foamed at the muzzle and Simeon felt the wing raking his leg. He brought down the butt of his carbine. He heard the bat's skull splinter. The wing leaped up and fell broken. Simeon drew back his shoe. Where the bat lay the ground sprang alive. In a moment the white maggots were at its belly and a dung beetle had its scissors in the dead wing.

90

Then he heard Amsel's cry and flinched from the wheeling blade.

— Stop that. Stop swinging that thing. You'll take my head off. They won't kill you.

The bats ripped loose from the tangle of hair and the flailing bodies. They swarmed through a break in the palm fronds and out of sight. Only their screech lingered and a randy smell.

Hitler made a warbling noise and said

— All clear.

— Put that thing down. You'll cut yourself.

Isaac heard his own cry and stopped, bewildered. The machete hung in a knot of tree moss and ferns.

— All clear,

said Hitler,

— finished. At sunset the Stukas go home.

But the raid had infected the march. A thrashing looseness possessed the legs and bodies of the six travelers. Even Simeon, who had taken the machete from the boy's flapping wrists and was again in the lead, heaved and stumbled forward breathing loud through his open mouth. He could hear the hiccups pummeling at Benassera's body and the sound drove him. Asher caught the scent of disarray, muskier than the fur of the tree bat. He knew that Simeon had altered course, that the sun, where it scorched through the tunnel of leaves, had slid abruptly from his left shoulder. But he did not halloo or ask Simeon for a reason. The urge to quit the swamp, the conviction that it would be death to spend another night on the gaseous slew harried the marchers. They kicked their raw stinking legs through the scum, slashed blindly at the shapes which rose and bobbed before their faces, each man laboring in the net of his own panic, in the wild fear of being left behind.

They moved fast, waist deep in a trough of gray mud, then through tassels of tree moss, the braids swarming with aninga beetles, armored creatures suspended by their precise claw.

— Thy works are manifold

said Elie Barach, and slogged on. Once Hitler cried out, pointing at Gideon,

— we must stop. That man has the fever. He will make us all sick.

But no one seemed to hear and Hitler hopped forward lest Asher, lurching through the creepers just behind him, stomp on his heel.

Toward evening the air lightened. Simeon felt a distant coolness, a puff of living breath on his lips. The wall of vegetation began thinning. The light steadied and for the first time since they had waded into the morass Isaac Amsel saw his shadow whole. The sapucaias and swamp sycamores drew apart. The water threaded into weedy channels; the green slick ebbed from their boots. Snapping a dry stalk, its top browned by the sun, Barach praised God. Soon they could hear one another's steps. The soughing of gas and oily water, the slap of vines, the blotted rasp of their own breath receded. A cicada sang bright as tin.

Twice Gideon tried to say

— wind, there's a fresh wind from the south

but his teeth were clenched against the fever.

Elie tripped and fell. His body was so worn that it lay like smoke on the coarse grass. He smiled and started to his feet. Simeon said they were almost out of the great bog and would halt for the night. Asher said he could smell fresh water. Beyond the stockade of trees the western sky was bright. The cockades of the calliandras seemed on fire.

— That man has the fever. He will infect us. He must be treated.

Simeon froze. It was the old voice. Now. For the first time.

— I know about the fever. That is how Körber died. I tell you that man must have rest. And quinine. And hot liquids. I tell you.

The old voice. It passed over them like a scythe.

— Look at him. If we catch the fever we will die. Just so.

92

Like the rats. We didn't have to hunt them. They gnawed their way into the hut. To get near the fire. And swelled up. Körber could swing them by his teeth. The tail between his teeth. But he caught the fever. You. Come and lie down here. Cover yourself up.

The voice as it had been, high pitched, incessant. Like a vampire's wing but heavier, bending their necks.

— That's right. Just so,

said Hitler,

— *so geht es besser*

as Gideon Benasseraf put down his pack and slumped heavily to the ground.

It took time to get the drug down his pulsing throat. A woman's fingers, thought the boy watching Hitler tap the powder into Simeon's palm, the fingers of an old woman. Now the shadows lay close; shapes grew indistinct in the light of the small flame. The hunters were too winded to pitch a tent and even here, at the edge of the swamp, the earth was like a sponge. Only Asher stood apart trying to make out, through the screen of toquillas, acacias and charred grass, the rise of the stars in the southern sky. They were off course, he supposed, by almost ten degrees But Simeon's back was to him, arched over the shivering, loud-breathing man.

— I tell you how it is. That man will die,

whispered Hitler,

— even if we reach help. Too late. The fever. It is in his bowels.

— Shut up, said Simeon speaking low,

— *Mund halten.*

The prisoner sidled away and fumbled at a button on his sere gray tunic.

The cane stalks cracked. Simeon glimpsed the gold in the otter's eye momentarily held by the fire. The wet scent hung on after the stalks closed. Asher found it difficult to read the constellations. Behind the tree fronds the stars flickered and melted out of shape. Somewhere out of the far south, out of the burnt pampa, clouds were piling up.

Barach pictured the fever as a lizard, a spiny quick thing free from its cage in Gideon's body. Through his swollen lids he watched it dart up Gideon's thigh and scrabble in his groin. Sometimes it shot its venom into Gideon's mouth; a trickle of saliva came from the corner of his lips. Elie Barach bent close, tensing his will, the love he bore Gideon, against the lashings of the worm. He reached into Gideon's flesh with the strength of his own stillness. When the body is at prayer it weighs more than cedar said Ithiel Ben Tov at Salamanca when the flames reached him.

The tremors lessened. Gideon's teeth opened and the vein in his temple grew flatter. Elie watched, immobile, his back like a strung bow.

— Elie. Elie.

Barach jumped. Had he fallen asleep? In the house of need? The fire was almost out and a blackness thicker than night towered in the south.

— Elie, is it you?

Gideon's eyes were open and fever-lit.

— Elie. Where are we?

— Almost out. Out of the swamp.

— Out? Too soon. We shouldn't be. Not yet. Not if we want to reach Jiaro. We're off course. We must be.

— Simeon knows. If we hadn't cut east, if we were still in there, we would never get out alive. Look at me. I fell down and sat like a sick child when we reached here. And you. God be praised we're out of that. Like being buried.

— Perhaps we should have. I mean we should have stayed in there. Guarding *him*. Keeping sleep from him. Keeping the wind from his face. He would have outlived us. But our bones would have kept watch. He would have died slowly in the circle of our bones. And not heard sleep again or the fresh wind. Do you hear it now? We are wrong to be out of the swamp. To be

94

out so quickly. Now he is asleep. Just like a man. The south wind. Do you feel it rising? I can almost reach it.

— Cover yourself. Try to sleep. Cover yourself, Gideon. When we're in Jiaro

— When?

— we'll have you well again. Soon now. But you must rest.

— Good as new, Elie?

— Better. Yes.

— I am tired. I am tired of me. Of the smell of me. In the swamp I knew where I was. And what he was. Now I.

The fever snapped at Benasseraf's wrist. On the blanket his fingers jerked open.

— Now Hitler sleeps like any man. He can look at the stars. That's all we've done. Look there. The red one low in the northeast. In the swamp he could see nothing. Only the yellow air and the stench on the water. Why go to Jiaro?

— Stay covered. You'll be on your feet soon. We'll have help. And cold beer. The way your toes stick out, Gideon. We'll get new boots. And soap. I want a thick bar in each hand. Lieber is waiting in San Cristóbal. Perhaps nearer.

— Lieber? Have you ever seen Lieber?

— Of course. That day on the ship. When you saw him. Of course I've seen Lieber.

— What did he look like?

— What did he look like?

Elie laughed or thought he had.

— Don't you remember? He was wearing glasses. The sun was like a knife. So he wore dark glasses. And a round hat. And an old raincoat with a belt.

— What was his face like?

— His face? Why, ordinary. Yes, perfectly ordinary. I didn't notice. Keep the blanket on you. It was dark in the cabin.

— Elie,

The noises of the bog were still loud in the canebrake and Elie Barach leaned nearer. His back ached and he wanted to rub it.

— Elie, said Benasseraf,

— about Lieber. Simeon knows who Lieber is. He's the one that needs Hitler most. Lieber. They need each other like the breath of life. Lieber couldn't rest, couldn't breathe till he was found. And marched out of hell to where there is light. It had to be done, and if our bones rotted on the way. Without Hitler where is Lieber? Elie, try to understand. I'm not brain-sick, not yet. A man strangling his own shadow. Because without Lieber there would be no Hitler. Not any more. Listen to me. Don't turn away. I don't say there would never be Hitler. Or have been. But not now, sleeping next to us, the stars over him as they are over you. That's why we haven't seen Lieber's face. Not the whole of it. Supposing they were, supposing.

Gideon's jaw quivered as the fever rose. Elie rolled the blanket under his armpits.

— I'm not saying. I'm not out of my head. But Lieber's need is a terrible need. It tastes of vomit. I don't want to see them. Not together. By the time you reach San Cristóbal I won't be alive. Don't shake your dirty locks in my face. San Cristóbal? I want no part of it. The job is done. We should stop here or go back into the swamp and there.

— We pray for the coming of the Messiah. Interminably. Somewhere in the world, at every moment, a Jew is calling on the Messiah, wailing for him to come, to hurry. But not every Jew. There are those, oh they are not many, and they are the secret ones, who whisper to him *not* to come. Who know that judgment and the end of time will be more dreadful, more hideous to man than all his afflictions. Jews are the lightning rod. God's fires go through them, into their roots. We are made ash. Through our cunning the Messiah is delayed. Lest His justice and His vengeance consume mankind. Lieber is one of the secret ones. Lieber

— Crap. Golden words. You make your bread of them. To you they smell sweet like your own shit. You sing to yourself. Even in the swamp. I heard you. When the rest of us were crazy

96

for water you drank words. The secret ones, the parables of the masters, the seventy-two Names of the Unnamable. Words. Air out of the furnace. We are the people of the word. That's what they call us isn't it? Well, listen to me O secret one,

— Don't, Gideon. Don't pull the blanket away. You're shivering.

— he too, *he,* the sleeper under the stars, he is a master of words. Greater than Hillel, greater than Akibah, greater by far than the thirty-six just ones.

— Try to keep warm. The night is turning

— Why there is nothing he could not do with words. They danced for him. They set fire to stone. They made men drunk or battered them to death. We talk too much, Elie. For five thousand years we've talked too much. Talked ourselves and the world half to death. That's why he turned on us, that's why he could tear the guts out of us. Because he too is a man who made words louder than life. He and us. He and Lieber. Oh such need of each other. A dog and his puke.

— You'll make the fever worse, said Elie Barach, and smoothed the blanket and the rubber ground sheet. They were soggy with dew. For a time Gideon said nothing. Then

— Elie, where are you?

— Here, Gideon. Right here beside you.

— The night is blacker, blacker than night. You see, I can talk like you.

— There are clouds behind us. They're mountainous.

— There were those who said

— Who said what?

— that he is one of us.

— A lie. A sick stupid lie.

— Every file burnt. The village where his father was born razed. The archives in Linz sacked the week after he became Chancellor. And a tombstone in Bucharest. The name Hitler under a Star of David. Adolf Hitler.

— Lies. Journalists' gossip.

— A tramp out of nowhere. An actor. A master of words. Look at his mouth, even when he's asleep, look

— There's nothing to see. It's too dark. Nothing. He has his arm across his face.

— it moves. He speaks in his sleep. An actor's mouth. A Jew's mouth. Like yours. The words crowding behind his rotten teeth. Making his teeth hum.

— He's got his arm across his face. You can't see his mouth. I can't see my own hands. Stay covered, Gideon. You're shaking.

— That is why he had to kill all of us. He could not rest so long as one of us was left alive anywhere on earth to recognize him, to say "welcome *Spieler*, word spinner, mountebank."

— All craziness. There is not a grain of truth in it. Fever and lies.

— How else could he have understood us so perfectly? Found us in the hidden places? Known that we would walk into the fire pit, with just a dozen butchers, lame men, dogs gone in the teeth, herding a thousand Jews, a hundred thousand? How else would he have known?

— Madness, Gideon. Fantasies. You must try to sleep. You must sleep off your fever. We must press on in the morning. Before the rains come.

And Elie Barach turned to look into the nearing blackness.

— To be the final Adam. That's what he wanted, the old *Spieler*. What's the use of being a Jew, one of the chosen people, if there are millions of others? That's nothing to shout about. But to be the only one left. The last Jew. Kill all the others. And be the last. World with end. Can you hear me, *shlemiel*? Your lips are moving. I know they are. Moving in the dark. You murdering ham.

In the ferns a rat's foot crackled.

After a while, perhaps longer, Elie said

— the Other Messiah,

He said it not to Gideon Benasseraf, short of breath under his sodden blanket, not even to himself, but under dim compulsion, as if to reach his own hands, two gray patches divorced from him in the airless, totally still blackness.

— the Second One, foretold by Malchiel. There shall spring from the seed of Abraham, from the tree of Jesse, absolute good and absolute evil. Light out of Jacob and dark. Only one of our number could have accomplished what he brought to pass. Only a Jew could make of the Jew a man halfway in the house of death. His lips *are* moving. Even in sleep he says the incessant prayer, the other *kaddish,* no one dared speak of it in *cheder,* whose one hundred and nine syllables bring death and the end of time. Hitler the Jew.

Gideon, now propped on his elbow, could not make out all of Elie's words but heard the desolation.

— Don't. Elie. *Petit frère.* Don't cry. I am talking balls. I've got a fever in my head. It's all nonsense, fantasy. A sick man playing games.

He reached out but Elie shrank away.

— Don't listen to me. I was talking stupidly. Just talking to keep my teeth from rattling. That one over there? A hooligan. A mad dauber. Shit-brown. He'll be off our hands soon. We'll hand him over and act sane again. Listen *zadik,* we'll go to the seaside you and I. Sit on a bench all day till the wind blows us clean. And say marvelous words like "What time is it" or "Stop picking your nose" or "Do you want chocolate ice or vanilla?" Words human beings use. Not the lofty poisonous *Dreck* we've been mouthing at one another in the swamp. Elie, don't cry like that. We're hysterical, we need a cold bath, the lot of us. I was saying anything that came through my poor head. Don't believe a word of it. It's lies just as you said, foul gossip. Him a Jew? And *so* stupid? To be caught by the likes of us? It's only that I thought that once we had him *everything* would be different. I don't know what I thought. That the stars would sing in their course, that's how it goes isn't it, and the moon stand still over Rio. That we would step out of our own stink and be like men reborn. It's all foolishness. Even if there is no light anywhere else, anywhere in this stinking world there should be light here so that I could see you *petit rabbin*. I don't know what I imagined. Fevertalk. But you've stopped whining. I can't get the taste out of my mouth, like cabbage and chloroform. Like the smell of the open pits at Orosso. Do you remember? You turned green as piss. Give me some water, Elie. I know it makes the fever come on. But the taste is driving me crazy. Have you ever tasted yourself, I mean in small bits? That's why I talk stupid.

And Gideon talked on in a hoarse murmur drawing on what he had left of friendship and foulmouthed ease. Until the thirst made his tongue stick.

— Come on, Elie. Give me some water. There's some left in my canteen. But Asher said there was a spring. I heard him say it. Elie. Can't you hear me?

Elie Barach sat hunched up, swaying a little. Gideon wondered at his soft breathing.

— You're fast asleep little brother. I'll have to get my own water.

As Gideon pushed back the covers and shuffled the poncho from his feet, a numbness took hold. He pulled himself to his knees and rubbed his leaden calves. The damp lay on him like a sack. Gideon lumbered to his feet but could hardly feel the ground. He extended his stiff arms to keep from falling. The dark spun slowly around him and he bent forward. His dry mouth labored.

— They're all asleep. *Les cons*. Asher said. He said there was a spring nearby. I need a fucking light.

Gideon lurched and spread his fingers as if the night had pillars to lean against. He shuffled toward the tall grass. He pounded his foot on the ground trying to get the blood going. Under the black towering clouds, thicker than walls, the air stood absolutely still. A branch snapped in the far heart of the swamp. Gideon staggered and beat his heel on the sodden earth. Out of his numbness came the fever, its blade edging up his spine. His body slapped against the reeds and the sound carried like a shot. His arms and legs were strangers to him, wild hammerers.

Gideon danced. The slow tottering dance of his fever. His drumming steps boomed hollow.

Beyond the sycamores and tagua palms, in the thornbushes which marked the edge of the scrub, the Indian froze. The white men had seen him melt away. But he had shadowed their tracks. Now Teku heard the drumming. And whispered to himself that it was madness, evil madness, to dance the rain dance when the clouds were coming on thicker than he had ever seen them, when they might, provoked by this false magic, swallow the earth. He looked up and gave a loud cry. The east was gone. Where first light should have been there was now a fantastic smoking blackness.

The night burst in the south. A wall of thunder higher louder than the great falls was boiling toward him. The dark raced at him in a blinding thrust. It slammed the air out of his ribs. Teku spun and ran for the trees. The first icy drop caught him in the neck. Then the cold black deluge was on him and he yelled for breath.

Gideon was still dancing. The earth steamed under his tread.

10

— Niiice

The pilot made three syllables of it, brushed his fingers across the amplifier and gave the rotary antenna a delicate turn.

— Very nice. A 207 range finder!

Appreciative, muted whistle.

— Haven't seen one of those before. Not mounted on a d-k circuit.

He flicked a switch. The blips came on dim, then contracted to points of humming brightness.

— I'm nuts about this stuff. I'm a radio ham. Just like you, Mr. Kulken. You've got yourself some nice hardware. The man's glance shifted. But bleeding Jeeesus what a dump.

Gathering her smock the Indian woman had, in motions amphibious, retreated to the far corner of the shack.

— No offense meant, lady. You got a nice place here I guess. But Orosso.

He had trouble with the word. It was new to him.

— Keerist, I've landed on some crummy strips in my day. But this field takes the cake. I almost cracked up taxiing in. And get a whiff of the joint. No drains?

The inquiry was solicitous.

— What kind of Indians you got here? I left one of 'em guarding the single. Gave him half a dollar. I told him I'd bust his ass if anything was stolen. That I'd skin his greasy hide. What kind of Indians you got, Mr. Kulken?

He moved closer. There was liquor on his breath, but not much.

— Goddamn bugs.

He slapped his forearm and peered thoughtfully at the squelch.

— Haven't you got any DDT Mr. Kulken?

Kulken was on his feet, his erection undermined. Who in hell are you? What do you want here? Who let you in? He couldn't have asked these stupid questions, couldn't actually have blurted them out, his cheeks rounded and sweating, in the bewildered stance of a grade-C thriller. Not Rodríguez Kulken who had in settings infinitely more tortuous, in imbroglios more sinuous by far, kept his cool, not unmasked his batteries. Perhaps it was the pajama bottoms that had precipitated him to so banal an exhibit of enraged wonder, the fact that he had not, in the haste of his rising, tied them properly and that they kept slipping from his shrunk but aching nakedness.

— Marvin Crownbacker. Pleased to meet you, Mr. Kulken. And the lady. But everyone calls me Charlie.

This time Kulken heard himself say "Why." Why Charlie? And the grossness of his query, the way in which each cliché of alarm made the ambush tighter brought sweat to his eyes.

— Goddamn it. The bugs around here. Like crazy.

The intruder swiped at his chin but the insect was gone.

— This is a hot town you've got here. You bet, Mr. Kulken. Why Charlie? Wish I knew. I was born and raised in Muncie,

103

Indiana. They've called me that since I was knee-high to a grasshopper. You call me Charlie, Mr. Kulken. It's friendlier that way.

And Marvin Crownbacker offered a warm crooked smile.

Kulken tugged furiously at his pajamas.

— What do you want? How did you get here? Get out of my house.

Which behest insinuated into Kulken's fuddled brain, with mournful, numbing clarity, the remembrance of a play seen long ago in a flea-ridden casino hall somewhere on the Belgian coast. The white-faced actor had cried "Get out of my house" and pointed his long index finger.

— I flew in about an hour ago. You must have heard me coming down. Mist was covering the whole valley. Like flying through clam chowder. I nearly peeled the roofs off looking for the strip. And the engine was hotting on me. Mr. Kulken, do you mind if I sit down?

Charlie swept from under the table the metal stool on which his host had, for the past three weeks, sat each night, his bones stiff as wire, plucking the cries and turnings of the hunt from the loud secret weave of the air.

— I'm a radio ham. This kind of gear bugs me. Just like you, friend. So how about a cup of coffee. I've come a long way to see you, *amigo,* a very long way.

He'll show his hand, thought Kulken.

Charlie did. Over three cups of coffee with three lumps of sugar in each, two fried eggs, their yolks faintly mottled as they invariably are in Orosso, and over a plate of seedcakes which the Indian woman, for all her brooding sloth, made beautifully. The gentleman from Muncie talked in a rush, his intimacies and casual foulness of speech like a smoke screen on a dun sea. The start of the affair was slippery. Charlie was a radio buff, oh not on Mr. Kulken's sumptuous scale, but pretty hot in his own small way. He had picked up some of the stuff Kulken had sent Montevideo and once or twice he had got a fix on the transmitter in the rain forest. Nothing like Mr. K.'s precisions and range but enough to put two and two together and find that they added up to—what shall we say?—a million, no make it two or three million bucks. Which wasn't hay whichever way you chose to look at it. So he'd high-tailed it down to San Cristóbal and hired an old crate of a Fokker, two-seater job, put in an extra fuel tank and flown to Orosso. The goddamn sewing machine had almost ditched him a hundred miles out of nowhere.

Where had he monitored Kulken in the first place?

Hadn't he said? He'd been in Brasilia, free-lancing.

The word was to cover zigzags of life and a body of knowledge sudden, cascading, remote from Kulken's but in whose confident jargon Kulken could recognize an appetite for expertise, a feel for the grain and yield of things matching his own. "When our friends hotfoot it out of the jungle (it must be hell's asshole in there) we'll be the first to say how-de-do, won't we Mr. Kulken?" They hadn't been doing much transmitting over the last days and toward the end their signals had been barely audible. "You bet you they're out of juice." Which deprivation signified that there was only one link with the outside world: "all that sweet circuitry of yours." Why, they were sitting on a gusher, sitting on it right this minute. They'd need a truck to cart the money to Fort Knox. It was, forgive the expression, the biggest piece of fuckin' good luck that had ever happened to Marvin Crownbacker and he was going to make sure that Mr. Kulken got more than his cut, say twelve per cent more, "seeing as to how you're Johnny-on-the-spot and got the old mike just waiting, pretty as can be." Because this was the biggest story of the century. Bigger than Lindbergh. Bigger than John Fitzgerald and welcome to Dallas the friendly hub. Bigger than Jonestown—and that had been a honey of a PR setup if Charlie had ever seen one. God almighty! this was the hottest news break since Jesus got off his slab. This was like being at tombside and getting an exclusive from Him on the way upstairs. A couple of million dollars? More, sir, perhaps more. First there'd be the interview with the old motherfucker himself. They'd have U.S., Canadian and world rights on that and all reproduction thereof, live, canned, videotaped. "How does it feel being back out? What were your first thoughts when you saw these gentlemen dropping in on you? Do you think they'll try you in Jerusalem like the other guy? Anything you want to tell the folks out there about life in the jungle? Any dietary problems? It's a while back, but now that they may hang you, any regrets? Any thoughts about how your mother would feel?" Let Mr. Kulken imagine it if he could. World rights on *that* with a hundred million people out there waiting to hear every word and a hookup on satellite. After which there'd be hour-by-hour flashes and feature fill-ins. What's he eating? How's he sleeping? A special word to the Krauts. An appeal to the Vatican. Who's going to be his mouthpiece at the trial? Then there'd be the good guys. How many did Mr. Kulken reckon there were? Three, four, half a dozen? Hadn't they been seen slipping into the forest? The full treatment for each man in the party: life story with serial rights (Charlie had brought along the contracts, the agent's release forms, the whole legal crap). Background stuff: what brought you here Mr. Cohn? How does it feel being a world hero? Was it the greatest thrill of your life, I mean when you spotted him? What will the missus say and the kids? You have a sweetheart in Tel Aviv? Okay, Mr. Kulken here will hook in a circuit and you can talk to her. All rights reserved. Charlie wasn't any Cartier-Bresson. But he'd taken along a couple of Leicas and a Graflex 400. They'd have the first pictures, the only pics for the agencies, at least during the first forty-eight hours. Any TV outfit wanting to show them would have to pay, through the nose. Two thousand for each individual snap, ten thousand for a group shot of old *Shitgruber* and the Rover Boys against a jungle background. Charlie had brought color film "so maybe we can throw in a few Indians." He figured they had forty-eight hours, maybe a bit more if they played it smart, once the party was out of the jungle. Two days before Orosso turned to Coney Island, before every goddamn journalist, cameraman and publisher from Kalamazoo to Ulan Bator came in by helicopter or GoKart. By which time

— they'll have to come to us, Mr. Kulken, 'cause we'll have the contracts, the sole and exclusive right to deal with and negotiate for the sale of subsidiary and other rights within all territories covered by said agreement, i.e. newspaper and magazine serialization, anthology digest quotation and abridgment, dramatic, film, radio and television, microphotographic reproduction and picturization, reproduction by phonograph records and other mechanical means whether by sight, sound or a combination thereof, translation into any foreign language and that, sir, includes Bantu, Toltec, Easter Island and/or Yiddish. If the publishers have not sold paperback rights two weeks after publication of the hard-cover edition or agreed to publish a paperback themselves, the said sole agents and representatives for the said motherfucker and our heroes will have the option to negotiate with a publisher of their own choice for said paperback edition the publisher's share then being reduced to fifteen per cent.

Some of which rights, especially to more recondite portions of humanity, Messrs. Crownbacker & Kulken, otherwise entitled C-K Universal, would resell, because greed was a vile thing and because they had no hankering to spend the rest of their affluent lives signing releases to Bushmen.

— Millions, pal, millions. Sweet Jesus above!

At which invocation the gentleman from Indiana surged out of his seat exultant, threw his head back and whipped a sugar cube into his mouth. But Kulken too was on his feet attempting a dry, superior laugh.

— You're crazy Mr. Whatsyourname. *Loco*. You have jungle fever, that's what you have. A million dollars? For an interview with Martin Bormann?

— Martin Bormann? Who's he? Who the hell is Martin Bormann?

The two men stared at each other. Crownbacker spat the sugar from his mouth and forced Kulken to his seat. He thrust his face close and spoke slowly. As to a very stupid or very cunning child.

— Listen to me, Mr. Kulken. Let's not waste time playing games. Listen to Charlie. He's your friend. When Adolf Hitler walks out of that jungle.

Kulken went white and sagged forward. Charlie yelled at the Indian woman in a voice loud enough to wake Manola at the other end of the village

— Get me a glass of water. Water you stupid bitch. *Agua.*

Kulken came around soon enough and shoved away the proffered mug. But he was shaking. The immensity of the proposal, the image it conjured up of his blind nonentity, of his flyspeck role in a web vast, consequential beyond even his own most flamboyant reveries, made him hot and cold and nauseated in quick succession. It *had* brushed the far edge of his mind as a fancy lighter, sooner dropped than dust; he *had* made some remark over the chill pungent soup in the Casa Popo to the effect "Who do you think they'll turn up, the old carpet chewer himself?" only to have his host (*now* he remembered that the man *was* more senior than any he had met before) frown at him with lordly distaste. The queer had kept him in the dark. No one had even hinted to R. Kulken, Esq. what the game was. A "routine snoop." Somebody's hobbyhorse in Whitehall. "A loose end worth tying up. Possibly. And only if Señor K. had nothing more pressing on his hands and cared to pick up a little something." Which was precisely what it was. A pittance. An infamous *pourboire,* grossly inadequate to the skull-splitting labor of the last weeks, but niggardly insulting, humiliating beyond belief when set beside the immensity of the stake. So they'd let him sweat his ass off for their own incalculable profit and glory. The last message. The sun standing still. Ajalon and Hosannah. They'd bagged him. Mother of God they'd gone into the green hell and found him. Now London knew and the jackals were on their way. The lean ones with the tight gray skins and the talcum powder. With accents like an open razor and a lemon in their teeth. To bugger him once again, to scratch him off like a dry scab while they pulled in the catch, the immeasurable dizzying prize.

— You okay, *amigo*? Take a deep breath.

But suppose Crownbacker was lying? Or mistaken, taken in by his own circus patter?

Kulken snatched at the possibility. He sat up and forced a condescending smile.

— Hitler? Hitler died a long time ago. Thirty years or something like that. It's Bormann they're after. Everyone knows that. You've come on a wild-goose chase Mr. Charlie.

— Have I, asked the man in the yellow leather flying boots, and gulped the last of the seedcakes.

Kulken nodded and made a gesture of dismissal. But he did not look at friend Charlie and his bent smile. The truth pressed on him. In school they had held him to the wall and set the point of a compass inches from his eyes. He needed time. Morning air to clear his beating head. Kulken remembered his pajama bottoms. They were soaked with perspiration. Crownbacker wasn't half as smart as he made out. If it really was Adolf Hitler. Why, that meant

and Kulken almost laughed out loud with a sense of insight, of a global perception far more sophisticated than the crude El Dorados offered by his unwanted guest.

If Adolf Hitler walked out of that jungle toothless, lame, blind, palsied, in any form, husk, shadow of his ancient self, there wouldn't only be press agents and candid cameras waiting. Crownbacker was a poor ponce if he really thought that. The thing was political, deeper than adder pits, more crammed with danger and occasion than anything Rodríguez Kulken had ever had a finger in. Even with the shakes and with the stinking pajama stuck to his private parts, Kulken could make out, as in a doorway suddenly darkened, a future of clandestine offers and handsome betrayals, of *razzie* and *conversazioni* in summit places

109

far richer, far better attuned to his, Kulken's, alchemy of life than all the vulgar loot dreamt up by Charlie boy.

Kulken drew a long voluptuous breath.

But the man had to be got rid of. Kulken needed time, a zone to maneuver in freely.

— Get out Mr. Crownbacker. I don't know what you're talking about. I don't know what you think you picked up. And what's more, I don't give a fart.

Charlie stood still. His eyes were a watery green. Kulken's voice rose.

— What the hell do you think you're doing barging into a man's house? Get out. Just like I told you. Shove it.

In her corner the Indian woman moved heavily.

— You asked me what kind of Indians we have here. I'll tell you mister. The kind I can whistle for and who can strip a plane so fine there won't be a bolt left. Beat it, and *buenos días*.

The American shook his head, gently, as if there had been some trifling error.

— I'm not going, Mr. Kulken. You know that. I know that. So why get in a lather? Anyway, I couldn't. Not now.

As Kulken rose at him Marvin Crownbacker moved away with a catlike spring. He kicked the door of the hut wide open. The morning was gone, eclipsed. Two streaks of yellow light smoldered on the wall of the outhouse. Beyond them, billowing toward Orosso, came a blackness high as the sky. A flogging sound was advancing through the forest, louder than the churn of the falls. The Indian woman clapped her hands to her mouth. The rains had begun.

— I couldn't leave now, partner, could I?

said Charlie.

11

"Reger. The Humoresque in B minor. She plays it well. Very well. But not brilliantly. Like everything she does. A barrier at the edge where feeling should flow free. Music equals freedom in time, freedom from time."

Gervinus Röthling took pride in his ability, achieved over years of unwavering alertness to the casual drift and anarchic insubordination of human consciousness, to think in an orderly fashion while listening to music. So far as Dr. Röthling was aware there were not many people who could do so. Music was the prime loosener; with it thought slipped its moorings and meandered in lethargic maelstroms over deeps of after-dinner ease. When Dr. Röthling listened fully, when he became "all ear," he voided the rummage room of his ordinary self of any intrusive awareness; he could make his soul silent, open-armed as death. But when he listened with only a part of himself, the precise degree of attention being one that Dr. Röthling could select, when he allowed a current of thought to flow as it were between the music and that compact node of identity which he guarded above all things, he saw to it that his reflections were orderly and complete. Not a halfway possession: to reflect, to feel without syntax while listening was to make of music an opiate, an aspirin for the elite.

"Music is freedom in/from time. All other human activities and sensations have in them a temporal axis. A linear thread of time sequence runs through them. But it is a thread from outside, from a system of coordinates already established and often alien to their nature. Even a dream, even a bout of delirium does not create its own time. It merely compresses or distorts an outwardly determined temporality. Time pulsates in a crystal and flattens space in the center of the galaxy. No reality is accessible to human understanding outside the *a priori* grid of time, says Immanuel Kant. No reality except one. That of music. Each piece of music whether it is the *Ring* or one of Webern's cello studies scarcely over a minute long re-creates time. It creates its own time, an expressive sequence unique and proper to itself. Other chronometries, that of the metronome, that of the actual time required for performance, are only marginally relevant. The true time of music is a construct interior to the particular composition. A piece of music *takes time* but not in the ordinary sense, not in reference to the clock. It sets itself across the general flow of time in which we conduct our regimented lives with a specific assertion of freedom so absolute as to dwarf other pretenses at liberty be they political, private, orgiastic. Music is the only reality perceptible to man that governs time. It draws out of our flesh that arrow of past-present-future implanted at the instant of birth and speeding away from us in outrageous anonymity at the moment of death. Each piece of music generates its own temporal sphere, its own alpha and omega of complete existence. When we listen to music we are at once within and wholly outside the banal sovereignty of our clocks. An inverse canon such as that of Tallis or the reverse counterpoint in *The Well-Tempered Clavier* I, 6, does what mystics dream of and addicts strive after by the use of drugs: they create time

112

systems which reverse themselves, in which the future, in the full concrete sense of thematic logic, can precede the past or in which two arrows fly in opposite directions yet remain parallel. When a man composes music, when he invents a melody—such invention, such passage from one plane of energy to another being perhaps the *ultimum mysterium* of human existence—he performs a rite of freedom like no other. That rite is the definition of music. It is that which makes music irreducible to language. In speech lies our slavery, our obeisance, manifest every time we use a verb, to the tyranny of tense. Speech compels us to submit our experience however intimate however ecstatic to the universal vulgate of time past, the blur of presentness and time future. In fact, our resort to the future tense is a feeble squib, a slingshot loosed at the fact of our inescapable, unforeseeable death. To speak is to swim and finally drown in the murky, inhuman because unmastered, river of time. In true silence there is no time, or at least a brief leap out of time. Thus it is through its silences that language comes nearest to music. *La musique est la liberté dans le temps.*"

When one changed languages was one doing the same as when one changed keys? Dr. Röthling was uncertain. But he had often felt the curious finality of French, its capacity to round off a movement of thought. He heard the closing pedal point of the Humoresque.

"She plays well, of course. An honest touch. But not brilliantly."

Anna Elisabeth Röthling glanced at her father. The intensity of his audience, the way in which even his fingers seemed to listen, always moved her strangely. She brushed her fine dark hair from the nape of her neck and played again. Schumann's Toccata in C major. It had an awkward passage for the left hand. Anna Elisabeth concentrated but her father's presence surrounded her like the walls of the study.

"The Schumann Toccata. Not one of my favorite composers. A genius, to be sure. But was he totally committed to music? A translator into music of other things. His music is a mask. There are other forms underneath. Words, theatrical bits, Clara's morning coffee. Does Anna notice that? Probably not. It isn't that she lacks technique or intelligence. But there is always a barrier. She is like the others, her whole generation. Circling on a lead rein round and round in the manège, never tearing loose. Not one of them shows any skin for the wind to blow on. They walk muffled. Why? They have led solid lives, warm and lit as this room. Some of them pretend that they are carrying our national burden, that the past lies on their shoulders and the blood on their forehead. Mere hysteria. Melodrama. Whoever was not in it can have no real knowledge of what it was like, of why we acted or did not act. Those who claim they feel remorse on our behalf are swindlers. They invested nothing of their own conscience in that terrible account. What right have they to draw on it? Any man can say *Auschwitz,* and if he says it loud enough everyone has to cast their eyes down and listen. Like smashing a glass in the middle of dinner. So easy to do if you were a child at the time or not even born. When you can have no idea of what it was really like, for most of us, for the decent educated class trying to survive on that other side of the moon. Go ahead, say Auschwitz, Belsen, what have you, put ash on your head, shake your fists in our faces and demand that we do eternal penance. There's a tidy sum in remorse, TV serials to be produced, books for the autumn trade. I have only one question, my dear young ladies and gentlemen: what would *you* have done, what fine words would *you* have cried out at the time? When the brown men stomped by, the bravest of us wet our pants. But I am letting my mind wander. Anna isn't like that, nor are her friends. They drink life in small sips with just a touch of sugar, thank you, and perhaps a dash of milk. As if there were only a little left in the pot. Like trapped miners saving air. They who have grown up secure, who have had everything.''

The monitor in Dr. Röthling's consciousness, that part of his attention which had, beneath or rather to one side of his ordered

114

stream of thought, been following the piece, signaled the proximity of the difficult passage. The left hand had to cross over. He voided his mind of all but response and smiled as the harmony, momentarily rent, almost out of control in a *salto mortale,* returned through a modulation of startling yet perfect logic to unison. Anna Elisabeth did not look away from the keys but Röthling fancied that his smile had reached her.

"Nicely done. But so little edge, so few risks taken. How they sit, the lot of them, their knees tightly pressed together. Her mother was different. Elisabeth was free as open water. When she moved through a room the light danced. Is it our fault? Have we taught them too much about the past or too little? Are they afraid it will happen again and think it best to go by the back stairs softly? How they ration themselves. Perhaps that's it. Perhaps we *have* left them very little. We drank so deep of history that there can't be much left in the bottle. By God we took a mouthful! The catkin bursting into bud at Bryansk, cold furry pellets filling the air after the sudden thaw. The dead horses in the gorge south of Mycenae stinking to heaven, but purple cliffs on either side of us."

Röthling recalled his thirty-six-hour leave in Delft in the autumn of '42 when he had taken men of his company on a tour of the sights, shown them the hunched postern through which William the Silent stepped into present death, and gone on alone after seeing his charges properly fed in an *estaminet* near the station.

"Two perfect rows of poplars, one on each side of the canal. The vesper bells rang from somewhere in the town. The sound and the fallen leaves came toward me down the dusky water. A moment out of time. Two bodies swinging high on the unbleached gallows by the roadside."

His column was dragging south out of Norway. The crows had been at the partisans' eyes and stripped their cheeks, but a spring light sharp as broken glass had caught the two faces. They were beautiful to look on, marbled, folded in sleep. He

115

remembered his first taste of Calvados in a tin measuring cup handed to him by—by whom?—another officer, a gunner with whom he shared a bunker outside Stralsund. An apple fire blazed inside him and the warm fog blanketed their stiff bones. Each time the Stalin organs loosed a barrage and the rockets lashed overhead the liqueur shook in the cup. *Les très riches heures*. To have heard Gieseking play the *Waldstein* in Munich, almost at the end. Despite brave efforts at ventilation smoke hung in the concert hall and an odor of fire and burst mains blew in through the gilt-and-stucco foyer. He had sat at the back of the stalls in a wheelchair, coffined from the hip down. The plush *couloir* was reserved for wounded military personnel, for invalid *Frontkämpfer* home from a front already smashed, fictitious. Feeling the hand of the young woman from the Auxiliary Nursing Corps on his shoulder, Gervinus had turned in the dark to make out her tall form. After the recital, in the brief mercy of an all-clear, Elisabeth had wheeled him back to the sanatorium, maneuvering the chair over blistered pavements and deep ruts to what was left of a garden pavilion. She was not as young as he had supposed. She had married at the outbreak of war, seen her husband on two furloughs and received news of his death outside Narvik during the easy war, the one before the real. The sirens had started again and she had stayed by him in the blacked-out room. She knelt by his chair. He edged the uniform cape off her shoulders and unbuttoned her blouse. Already then, as they slipped behind her back to undo a hook, he had noticed how alive her hands were. He found her breasts. Their weight startled him. An old warmth came up in his broken thighs. Just then a stick of incendiaries splattered the branches in the far corner of the park. In the abrupt white sheen beyond the blackout draperies he saw how near her face was and that she had let her skirt slide to the quivering floor.

"I drank deep that night. As everybody was trying to do all around us, in open places in the crazy houses with no windows, no roofs. I let go. Of everything. As one can when death is no longer private, no longer one's own business."

She had left her mouth on his trembling arms until sleep came. Would he rather have lived in some other time in some other land? Would it have been better to miss the long holiday in hell? That was what they were saying now, making pious faces over the horror of it. It was a lie or only a part of the truth.

"I Gervinus Röthling have emptied life not from a glass but from a magnum. Have known history as I know my own skin. Have crossed and recrossed Europe like Napoleon's hordes, have seen Salonika burning and the face of an old man floating, smiling in the Grand Canal. I have smelled new wheat in the Carpathians and eaten eel, fresh, salt-cold from the Tyrrhenian sea. I have passed my hands over the stone roses in the cloister at Albi and over a woman's hair in a cellar in Kharkov. A magnum, a Jeroboam, till it was empty. I wouldn't trade. I wouldn't put my memories on sale or flaunt them like leprosy. God how we lived! Each terrible year like a hundred ordinary years, like a thousand. He was true to his word. A thousand-year Reich inside each of us, a millennium of remembered life. We have left nothing for those who came after. That's our real crime. They are ghosts, plump ghosts, lean ghosts, the whole generation of them. Not their fault. We left them the cold ash of history, the skin of the grape. But I wouldn't trade. I wouldn't."

Dr. Röthling came to with an unpleasant jerk. The music had stopped. He had let his thoughts run loose. For a bewildering instant he stared at the young woman in the room without precise recognition or rather with a queer pang of desire, observing the fullness of her shape, the full breasts turned toward him. Anna Elisabeth was smiling.

— I think you have been dozing, Papa. Was I that bad?

— Of course not. I have been fully awake. You took the difficult bit, the one for the left hand, well. Excellently, Anna. A little more bite, perhaps. Yes, that's what's needed.

117

He was talking too rapidly, trying to clear his head of a bizarre, numbing exultation. He flushed at the remembrance of the unseemly lust which had seeped out of his past.

— I should like a cup of coffee, Anna. A cup of strong black coffee would be just right.

As Anna stood up from the piano and pressed the bell button by the door, Röthling glanced around the room. Everything was back in place, the book-lined alcove, the ivory paper cutter which F. had sent him from Bengazi, the photograph of Elisabeth in its heavy silver frame, taken only a year before her death when a disorder of excessive life had already made itself felt in her body and carved hollows under her eyes. (At the clinic Rademacher had said: "My dear Gervinus, we all suffer from some form of cancer; anyone who has gone through the Hitler years carries inside him a heightened, anarchic life force. What shall we do to house the pathological energies and powers of adaptation loosed within us during this insane decade? Cancer is an unfocused excess of life, no more and no less. Your wife's illness is merely the most visible type.") Suddenly, as if it had been stored in some lone oasis of the mind, the close of the Toccata, the last modulation and final chord sounded in his ear, vibrant and distinct, as if Anna were still at the keyboard. "A trained memory is a wondrous miser" thought Dr. Röthling, shivered a little and straightened up in his cavernous armchair.

Over coffee they talked. Elisabeth chafed at the petty encumbrances of her job at the *Staatsbibliothek*. But was this plaint, her father wondered, more than conventional, more than a figured bass above which the young woman led her essentially harmonious, satisfied existence? That contentment, though muted, had been present even on a late afternoon in Ascona when, during a holiday they had taken together, Anna had stood on a ridge, with the western sky turning mauve, and declared her unalterable intent to resume her lapsed study of Russian, prepare her *Staatsexamen* and launch on a fuller course. At that hour her

118

resolve had been such as to draw her whole being toward the darkening horizon. But soon her resolution subsided, as had so many precedent gusts of high purpose, into that discreet nostalgia which was so clearly a part of her charm.

There was Thaddeus Binswanger, her immediate superior, with his spinsterish foibles and catarrh. Only this morning he had had a scene with Fräulein Schalktritt the archivist. Their voices had spiraled to such a *forte* of officious snorts and falsettos that Anna had sped from her desk and closed the door to the reading room. But it was not the occasional fracas which fretted her nerves (at bottom Miss Anna Elisabeth found vulgarity rather compelling); it was the monotony, the snail-pace hours she spent behind the high gray windows, especially now that the chestnut trees were dropping their glory and the afternoons were turning to smoke and fine rain. In the Library winter seemed to come a little earlier than anywhere else. She could tell by looking at the bust of Humboldt in the north corner; after three o'clock the plinth stood in a pool of shadows. She must pull herself together and look to other opportunities, that was certain. But it would be wrong, almost indecent to quit before the new children's section with its gay linoleum and adjustable reading lamps (her own idea, carried through in the face of Binswanger's carping and Miss Schalktritt's petty treasons) was properly installed and in use. To which resolve, so comforting in its indistinct futurity, Dr. Röthling vigorously assented, adding that the New Year was an excellent time for a fresh start, "for a thorough dusting inside," a mood which the coming season's municipal concerts with their rich sprinkling of Beethoven and Mahler could only reinforce. He whistled with that exactitude of pitch she envied the trumpet call from Mahler's Second. The clarion echoed around the room and died away in the magenta draperies.

Such was their intimacy that Gervinus Röthling and his daughter could fall into a kind of shorthand, grasping each other's intimations perfectly while eliding those connectives, prefatory signals and otiose stresses which make our ordinary use of speech so wasteful. Thus when Anna Elisabeth pondered her father's sudden inquiry

— Tell me, my dear Anna, what would you do if Adolf Hitler walked into the room?

the reason lay not in any vulgar surprise or confusion at so unheralded a theme but simply in her wish to give the matter due scrutiny.

— I should get up, said Anna Elisabeth,

— yes, I should certainly get up from my chair.

This interested her father.

— Why?

— Not out of common courtesy. Not to do him honor, God forbid. Perhaps out of shock at actually *seeing* him. But that's not it really.

She paused.

— If a man walked in who had loomed so large, so enormously in the lives of others, who had drawn to himself such a fantastic mass of hate, of love, of fear, simply of daily thought . . . I don't know that I can explain it. But how could one stay seated if such a terrible fullness of life, in him of course but even more in others, came through the door?

Röthling lit an English cigarette. He had developed a taste for them during his brief internment in a POW stockade near Hanover. He associated their grainy flavor with survival and the possibility, so remote in the last hellish weeks of the Reich, of thinking in the future tense.

— You mean that decent folk don't stay on their bottoms in front of history?

— Something like that. But you know I'm no good at putting things in precise words. You remember the time in the mountain railway, when we were going up the Schwarzhorn with Mother and someone thought they heard an avalanche far off. Everybody got up. Some were trying to see out the frozen windows. Others just stood listening, not to that bit of thunder so far away.

But stood. One couldn't just sit in one's chair and look up at him could one?

— And you'd curtsy, Anna, wouldn't you? The way you used to in school, just a very small curtsy.

— Certainly not, Papa. What an idea.

She flushed at the recollection, both awkward and somehow consoling, of how she had curtsied to Herr *Studienrat* Probst when he called her out of class and told her to put on her long blue overcoat and go home because Frau Dr. Röthling, because Mummy had taken a turn for the worse. She had raced through the streets full of March light and a new wind.

— Of course I wouldn't! But what would I do? Just stand there like a mesmerized goose? I couldn't touch him, I couldn't bear to do that. Spit in his face, call him foul names, take your knife and fling it at him? None of that sounds right. I don't think I could do any of those things.

Trying to enter the game, Anna Elisabeth found her resources meager and the image of herself out of focus. She stopped talking and stared at her empty coffee cup. After a while she shrugged faintly and looked up at her father. She resented his untroubled mien.

— Have they given you the file again?

Dr. Röthling nodded. It had, in fact, happened every few years. A thick intractable dossier on the juridical aspects of extradition and arraignment, on the competence of the courts both *Länder* and Federal, on the question of national vs. international jurisdiction in the eventuality that Adolf Hitler, sometime *Reichskanzler,* be found alive outside the territories of the German Federal Republic, the which territories had been held to include—held most emphatically by Röthling's lifelong friend, patron and predecessor, the late *Staatsprokurist* Gerlach—to include all lands proclaimed *Reichsdeutsch* up to and explicitly including the *Anschluss* of 1938. A point about which Gervinus himself felt intermittent but mournful doubts. It was, he deemed, a file whose convolutions, proliferating codices, minority reports and thousand-page addendum made in the murky light of the Eichmann affair he now knew better than any other man alive, in whose ghostly landscape he could thread his way as could no other member of the *Landesgericht,* let alone an outsider (and that included his esteemed correspondent, Sir Evelyn Ryder), could ever hope to. There were no doubt similar files at The Hague but less complete, less omnivorous in their imaginings of possible circumstance (i.e. let us suppose *ex hypothesi* or as Ulpian put it *per tentare lex* that the said A. Hitler be discovered on the high seas, on board a carrier flying a flag of convenience and holding Liberian registry, or in Vatican territory, in some country not party to the International Court, in a locality under disputation such as the nether reaches of the Argentine-Chilean frontier, the northeast corner of Basutoland or in the former German lands beyond the Oder-Neisse). No, the prodigality of conjectured happening, the ramifications of invoked precedent and counterexample docketed in his file were such as no other legal body could hope to equal.

They had asked him to refresh his knowledge of the whole matter and minute any views additional to those he had already set down in a series of memoranda since Gerlach's retirement and that disorderly escapade in Jerusalem—not that the Israeli case for *main haute et forte* had been quite as weak as some of his vociferous colleagues in the *Länderamt* and Ministry of Foreign Affairs would have it.

— Why had he been given the file now? asked Anna leaning her head to one side. It was a gesture which reminded Röthling of her mother, but Elisabeth's neck had been more svelte.

Instructions had come from Bonn marked *urgent*. There was always someone in that Ministry throwing his weight around. Rumors that Herr Hitler had been found alive cropped up regularly after the war. In more recent years Dr. Röthling could recall at least two false alarms (one of which alleged that the *Führer* had had himself circumcised and was now to be seen in an old-age home in upstate New York). Remnants of the onetime

Israeli search organization, tiny groups of individuals probably half-crazed and privately commandeered were thought to be operating still in the Amazonian hinterland hunting for Bormann, Menhardt or whomever they could flush from cover of the long register of vanished killers. So much was established. The rest had always proved gossip and astrologers' *Tratsch*.

— Surely it's impossible that he should still be alive. Even if he did escape from the bunker.

No, it was not impossible. Dr. Röthling begged to remind Anna that the Federal Republic had been governed after the war and, might he add, "governed in exemplary style" by a man almost as old as Adolf Hitler would be even now. But it was, to say the very least, unlikely. The so-called evidence of an escape from Berlin had never stood up to serious examination. The theory of a double was probably as nonsensical now as it had been during the *Führer*'s lifetime. Gervinus had caught a glimpse of the man once bestowing decorations and hoarse inaudible condolences in a military hospital on the eastern front. It was he, there could be no doubt. The sallow drawn skin was his and the rimmed eyes. Nevertheless this latest report had a queer insistence or at least it had produced distinct ripples in high quarters. Ryder was said to be interested; there had been two top-secret signals from Washington and the usual vulgar flap in Pankow. Only the Russians had let it leak that they regarded the whole affair as a boring canard.

— And what do *you* think Papa?

— That there's nothing in it.

Though it was not Röthling's concern, his old friend Berndt Dietrich had been helpfully indiscreet. A series of short-wave messages, the last fragmentary but exultant, had been emanating out of the jungle and half-explored swamplands beyond Rio Branco, wherever that was. The only curious feature was that so flimsy an affair should be taken at all seriously, that it should have provoked so marked a reaction in various nerve centers. Not that that proved much. Dr. Röthling's wartime experiences suggested that intelligence services manufacture news where there is none.

— Though from my own point of view the whole business is not, I must admit, unsatisfactory. You will remember, my dear, I am sure you do remember the strong reservations I expressed when the Munich courts pronounced Hitler dead—*re* the estate of Paula Hitler the alleged deceased's next of kin. I said at the time, the records will show how emphatically I said it, that such a declaration was either superfluous or premature: superfluous in view of the attestations of demise made jointly by the four-power Commission of Liquidation in Berlin, yet premature, from a more rigorous and forensic point of view, in respect of the absence of incontrovertible proof. I argued at the time, an argument, if I may say so, of some theoretic and even metaphysical import, that it would be far better to invoke the doctrine of *ratio mortalis,* of reasonably expected span of mortal life, and not proceed to any final certification of death until that length had been wholly exhausted. In brief, I proposed that biological truth be set in place of missing legal evidence. But the gentlemen in Munich would not listen. They were in a hurry. Now there's a pretty kettle of fish. Questions of extradition, indeed of our participation in any preliminary inquest or process of legal identification become somewhat thorny when the person involved has been declared well and properly defunct! Even if there is nothing in the present rumors, and I agree with you, Anna, that there really can't be, the Munich judgment will have to be reviewed. The law makes no provision for phantoms, for those who, as our French friends so nicely put it, "come back." I've drafted some notes on the matter and asked Rolf to drop over and discuss one or two points. He should be here any moment.

Anna Röthling smiled. Rolf Hanfmann's perennial courtship was more real to her father than to herself or, she supposed, than it had ever been to Rolf. How safely they had agreed to postpone any official betrothal until after Rolf's completion of his legal studies. How right it had seemed to them both that nothing save tacit understanding should bind them during Rolf's year at Oxford and that their engagement, pledged almost casually here in this room in her father's smiling but somehow edgy presence, should remain strictly a family concern until Rolf felt that his career had reached a requisite level of income and stable prospects. That was well over a year ago. Now Rolf's regular calls and presence on the Röthling agenda had an *obbligato* quality. The tall bespectacled young lawyer was to be her father's successor as he was already his assiduous adjunct. Perhaps something might come of it after all but it no longer seemed to matter very much and in the meantime the mild tension that came with Dr. Hanfmann's visits, the touch, so subdued, of frustration and unspoken reproach that intruded on their frequent meetings was, itself, not unpleasant. Certainly her father seemed to find it so.

As Rolf entered, a quick warmth tinged Dr. Röthling's cheeks. Anna saw that both men wanted to get on with the sheaf of papers which Rolf pulled out of his briefcase (she had given it to him on the evening before he left for England and remembered the feel of the monogram, newly incised, under her fingers). After a few minutes she gathered the coffee cups and said good night.

Röthling noted with pleasure how entirely Rolf had mastered the points he had put to him that afternoon, how closely his own vein of argument and even turns of phrase were reflected in Rolf's amendments or additions to the draft. Between them they would have the proposed abrogation of the Munich ruling and a further appendix dealing with certain vexed aspects of Adolf Hitler's Austrian nationality ready in a matter of days. It was at his mentor's invitation, conveyed by the fact that Röthling lit a fresh cigarette and leaned back expansively, that Rolf Hanfmann ventured beyond the immediate brief.

— I know it won't surprise you, sir, if I say again that there might be a case here for a more striking procedure. The indictment is necessarily without genuine precedent. This allows us to consider the institution of a unique court. I don't only mean

125

an international tribunal—there is nothing new in that. I mean, for example, a court in which those of us who had no direct part in the events, who were too young at the time or indeed unborn, could have a role to play. The accused stands outside the norms of law either common or specifically promulgated. Beyond any aim of judicial retribution—imagine, sir, how old the man must be if he does exist at all, how absurdly beyond correction—there is the hope that things can be got right. Facts, I mean, not motives. It is not so much a high and solemn bench we need as we do a school open to the world.

The young man's warmth of feeling, his bias toward the large and philosophic contour of things did not displease Dr. Röthling but the implication of a reality beyond the relevance of law could not pass. Either the law is an ontological totality both central in human institutions and capable by internal logic of extension to all human phenomena or it is merely and inevitably a corpus of local ordinance, an ephemeral fiat in this or that corner of history. Even as rights of eminent domain, of safe passage, of territoriality could be extrapolated to the deeps of the sea and the outermost reaches of interplanetary space, so a legal code covering murder, the ravage of property, the breach of constitutional oaths must be capable of extension to the case of the sometime *Reichskanzler*.

— If the codex does not apply to Herr Hitler, *Junge*, then he was absolutely right in claiming that he stood above the law, that the law is a bundle of mouse-eaten parchment with no authority over the superman or the will of the *Volk*. You are arguing nobly, I grant you, but most dangerously. I can conceive of no instance in the entire history of criminal pursuit in which it is more important that the forms, traditions and nuances of legality and judicial procedure be fully invoked. History has too long been extralegal, the atrocities which despots and nations commit have too long enjoyed immunity in some special fictional zone of "inevitable fact." There are laws, dear boy, not laws of history.

126

History is man-made, like this pair of shoes, though it pinches more.

— You, best of anyone, know my reservations in regard to Nuremberg. *Post facto* law badly drafted and argued. But the underlying truth was there nevertheless. If there is a law for the drunken homicide down the street there must be one for Attila.

Rolf did not dispute that. But the crimes of Attila were not really those of one man. This was even truer in the case of Hitlerism. It was not for those of his generation to judge— "What right have we, what qualifications?"—but manifestly the rise and deeds of Nazism involved the active support, the initiative of many other men, perhaps of millions. It was the relationship of Hitler's person to that support, the way in which he obtained and harnessed it, the question of whether responsibility could ever be localized which needed clarification. Could existing law do the job?

— I answer Yes, my dear Rolf, a hundred times Yes. And what I have in mind is no recent doctrine, no *ad hoc* psychologizing or supermarket sociology such as some of our esteemed colleagues in Bonn seem to favor. Your objection is met by a concept of *Staatsrecht* older than our Minister, by a body of legal thought

Gervinus Röthling came forward in his chair.

— richer, more subtly flavored than old *Traminer*. I refer of course to the concept of the *corpus mysticum* of the ruler, to that solid fiction so admirably worked out by our *Hohenstauffen* and their jurists whereby the identity and liability of the body politic is taken to reside in the body of the monarch. There is in him a twofold being, a duplicity of life: the one private and mortal, the other collective and if power be legitimate, eternal. During the period in which the sovereign reigns the earthly is joined to the transcendent in a perfect *incorporation* at once mystical and down to earth. It is not poetry, Rolf, that has produced the most vivid fictions or complex metaphors! A mystic carnality of state-

127

hood subsists even in the sleeping king; a *deus absconditus,* distasteful, perplexing to vulgar common sense as that may seem, endures in Hitler drugged or even demented. There is nothing in the difficulties you raise which old Henri de Bracton would have found surprising or outside the exact anticipations of the law.

In celebration of which fact Dr. Röthling poured a generous snifter of brandy for himself and young Hanfmann. But Rolf shook his head slowly. He acknowledged the force of his master's logic, he always did, yet was left dissatisfied. To him and doubtless to most other people in the world Hitler had become unreal, a specter trundled out on Halloween. The judicial machinery envisaged by Dr. Röthling would bring him no nearer. There was, however, no need to push the argument any further because

— we surely agree, don't we sir, that these latest rumors are unfounded, that the thing is well-nigh impossible.

— Quite. I can tell you, in strictest confidence of course, that the very location of the purported transmitter is in dispute. Some of our intelligence wizards think it's in Madre de Dios, on the Bolivian side. Others are confident that the messages come from the Ipiruna basin in Brazil. Moreover if this were a clandestine search operation why should the party, unless they all are brain-sick, use so transparent a cipher? As you say the whole affair is probably a fairy tale. How refreshingly sober our own trade is.

On the downstairs landing Dr. Röthling reminded Rolf that Bonn wanted a draft text as quickly as possible.

— Though in my humble opinion there is absolutely no ground for haste. My old friend *Staatssekretär* Dietrich tells me that the rains have begun in that God-forsaken part of the world. Not rains such as we know them, my dear Rolf, but black cataracts streaming down for days and nights, stripping giant trees, turning parched dust into a foaming lake. During the rains no one gets very far. The Indians hole up and drug themselves into a long stupor. Not a patch of sunlight for days. So I don't imagine

128

there'll be much news out of there for a while, if ever there was any. But that's Bonn for you. First they make a hash of things, then they're in a great hurry.

Röthling showed his guest to the door. The last strokes of eleven had rung from the *Domkirche* and the sound seemed to reverberate along the pavement. Röthling looked past the raw contours of the new concrete apartment buildings. In the moonlight above the sheen of the arc lamps rose the mitered crest of the belfry and the high roofs of the old city only partially burnt during the raids and scrupulously restored long since. It seemed to him that the night air in the thinning beeches made precisely the same drifting sibilant noise as it had in his boyhood. Unthinking, Dr. Röthling found himself clasping Rolf's shoulder.

— Things haven't changed all that much have they? Despite the bombing and all the rest. This whole Hitler business, perhaps one exaggerates its importance. Perhaps it's nonsense, a kind of upside-down sentimentality, to think back on it, to worry about how or why it happened. Like a terrier scratching for old bones. People who do too much of that go queer, they think they're making deep and terrible statements on behalf of the dead. They aren't. They're puffing up their own little lives. Oh it was hell; we were in it up to our eyes—while it lasted. And for a few years more. You can't remember, you were a baby. But now, looking back, don't misunderstand me, *Junge*, I can't help wondering whether it was very important.

Closing the front door—that sound too had scarcely changed since first he had tripped up the stairs of his parents' house, lacquered pumps in hand after the *Juristenball*, was it forty years ago?—Gervinus Röthling murmured to himself that proportion was the supreme virtue.

— Measure is the final aristocracy of man.

He said it aloud in the dark stairwell and wondered, as he neared the warm light of his bedroom, whether he was quoting one of Lichtenberg's aphorisms or, perhaps, one of his own.

129

12

Teku smelled them. Through air so sodden it hung before him like fur. The rains had driven him north. Much farther than he had ever been. The blackness and the winds had been crazy, blinding him, almost splitting his skull. He had been swept downriver and had clawed his way to the loosening banks when he had heard the thunder of the falls, a second thunder inside the drumming wind. He had had to keep moving to stay alive, to escape the racing sheets of floodwater. Scissored in the akuba trees, trying to fight sleep and the fetid cold, he had heard animals hump past in a crazed wallowing. The rains had lightened, but he was stunned and uncertain of his bearings. Who were these men? A Brazilian patrol, one of the minute fistfuls of armed men being flung far into the interior to mark future roads? Free-lancers lost from an oil or rubber party? They smelled like Sr. Kulken, only worse. Their lean-to had been punished by the storms, the leaf fronds carelessly joined and now gaping. But they had not been camping long in this spot. Teku considered the ash and the footmarked grass between the shelter and the high scrub. Two days, three at most. They must have run before the rains as he had. Stinking devils. How many? He moved his head in a tight arc, shaking the rain dreams, the panics, toward his left ear, whence they would spill once the sun was fully risen. His sight cleared. Two men at the east point, against the new light; a boy near the fire; a third man hunched by the hut, trying to steady a pole, wasting motion because the earth had not been properly tamped. Teku grinned and rubbed spittle against the scar above his left nipple. It smoldered after rain. As it was purposed to, calling up the pain of the great thorn and the rasping of the magic men in the long hut when he, Teku son of the anteater, had been made adult. Three men and the young one shivering by the fire. Ghosts rather than men, so sere the light seemed to go through them. Sr. Kulken was dense as a sow. Even his shadow weighed.

But where was the crazy devil who had danced the rain into its fury, and where was the old man? Because Teku's brain had awakened and the numbness was passing from him, to the left, as must the tree frog when he follows night. This was the same party, hunters or rubber tappers or men sick in the head, whom he had surprised at the edge of the great bog just before the skies had hammered down. He moved closer. The boy was not only shivering. There were tears on his grimed face. Teku parted the clotted grass and studied the whole site. He had been a fool not to observe at once, the rain had addled his wits. It was a poor piece of work; even the coypu would dig it up. A small barrow of earth where the ground was still drinking. No platform, no vines plaited to keep mud in place till it settled in the sun. You could almost make out the dead man's shape under the mound, his feet pointing eastward. Those dancing feet and torn boots. Teku shivered at the memory. Had the rains doomed him for his presumption? Had he died on the march here, somewhere in the intervening floods and ripped savanna? The carbine had been planted in the grave, its stock silhouetted against the sharpening light. How many guns did they carry, wondered the Indian, and felt his cheeks tighten. Then he saw the old man, in the entrance to the lean-to, bent, blinking into the morning. His skin was like that of a dried marmot or of a woman after famine. Teku was not certain whether he had ever seen anyone so old, not even among those who were now speechless, who crouched in the sacred hut inhaling the crushed seeds and who were thought to have seen the shadow of the gods.

— How do you keep the thread

Compacted as they were, each enmeshed in the others' needs and smells, so often out of breath or their mouths fouled with insects and lianas, Simeon, Elie, Gideon, John Asher and the boy had come to grasp one another's meaning, through half sentences, through words truncated by the slap of vines. But Asher had fallen short of a final immediacy. There were nuances which eluded him, elisions that had to be filled in later. He knew almost no Yiddish: "You are a dumb *shlemiel*" Elie had said, "the ox sits on your tongue." He had not experienced the Holocaust, but had been a schoolboy at the time in England, where green lay open as the sea and was not, as here, a sweating rag against the light.

— unbroken? You are connected to the outside world. Still.

Asher considered.

— The rest of us. What's left. I suppose we're more or less off our heads. The way we talk. As if Elie had dreamt us, made us up of a piece out of one of his parables. I can't picture the outside any more. Not since we have found him. And now Gideon dead. Crazy talk, isn't it? But you.

It was almost accusing.

— It still relates, doesn't it? I mean the politics, if we get to San Cristóbal. The people out there. Not only Lieber. The press, the microphones

and saying the words Simeon trailed off, mesmerized, then vacant.

— You've kept the thread. What's that story, the man in the labyrinth unwinding a strong thread and finding his way out again. You haven't tangled it or let it snap. Not on the thorns, not in the swamp. You're a careful man, John. Get him out, and the boy.

The sobs were strangled but audible. Simeon stole a glance at Isaac.

— He'll manage. He's lucky. Not every man loses two fathers, both heroes. And friend Hitler. You've noticed, haven't you. Getting stronger somehow, walking better, keeping his bowels open, brushing the fever from his skin while we

Asher had noticed. Outwardly the prisoner had withered. Even out of the wind his clothes flapped. The rains had whipped through him as through loose straw. But he had been gaining stamina, tapping recondite strengths as his escort sickened. When the fever hollowed Gideon's bones, making that tempered, adroit body a shambling, smelling wrack, the old man had looked on with gloomy interest, prescribed arrowroot and hellebore and had prognosticated, with a fair measure of precision, the moment of final convulsion. The vampire bat. He would make it out of the jungle leaving their bleached carcasses behind. Asher dwelt on the thought.

— The *rebbe* and I don't have anything to do out there. Not after this. I've heard that often it isn't the fire which destroys, but the water they pour in. Fire stains fade. But the water and the smoke soak in. So that the room feels dank years after. And has a dead smell like Elie and me. Not all the perfumes of Arabia. *Nebish,* Arabia. Did you learn the line in school? This little, little hand. You must have. At Bishop Romney's Grammar School in Hertfordshire. All in Lieber's file. He made me recite those files till I knew them blind. A dossier on each one of you, down to the final millimeter of past and private life. And then he incinerated the lot, so that no one would know or follow up. Melodrama.

Simeon said the word twice more, testing his rage and the emptiness.

— Melodrama. What was it like? I mean in Hertfordshire.

Asher translated. "Who are you, really? Why did you vol-

133

unteer, bulling through every impediment, setting aside every implausibility? And why, after everything we've been through, are you not one of us, not in the ways that matter?'' The same question, since the first night in Wiesenthal's study in Vienna all those wasted years ago. Then on the interminable, absurdly clandestine by-paths which led to Lieber. Every hour thereafter, until Genoa—even there, in the cabin, when Lieber turned to go, having voiced benedictions and auguries under his breath yet looking up suddenly, once again, with his flat eyes, to try to read on Asher's face the elusive meaning of his presence in the affair. The answer always the same, and straightforward enough. A man could be of use precisely because he was intact, because he had no true grounds for possession. He was one in whom interest was stronger than love or hatred or hunger. ''To be interested in something'' to the limit of one's stretched being, to be interested *in extremis*. The problem being enough to fill every cranny of the day. An algebraist's voracity. Asher had noticed his capacity for absolute appetites early, in the misery of home after his parents' divorce (the mixed marriage whose improper pairing made him technically, legally, Talmudically a gentile, though it was to the father, abruptly denuded, that the boy had gone on school holidays and most Sunday afternoons, in Ladbroke Grove where the leaves drifted). A capacity for orderly drowning. In a schoolboy craze, later in lepidoptera, later still in ordnance survey maps. Concentrations so knotted that they left the world to one side. Sometimes at the level of a parlor trick: extracting cube roots mentally to prevent erection. But gathering subconsciously, out of loose bits of reading, puzzling, devouring old newsreels, toward a master theme. The capture of Bormann and then, sprung from a rumor, from a tangential allusion heard during his stint in Army Intelligence, the lunatic notion of tracking Hitler himself. A passion as total as Gideon's had been. But rooted in the brain, irresponsible to anything but the vexation of the problem, autistic. It was this passion he had proffered his questioners, together with a marksman's skills, attainments in mountaineering and cross-country, an insolent ease at languages. No metaphysical lusts, no cravings for retribution. And they had finally included him because the laws of coherence in a distant patrol demand delicate asymmetries. Being an outsider to Lieber's monomania and the raging hurts it woke in Simeon or Elie or the boy, being, rather, monomaniacal but in his own hedonistic guise—"this, Mr. Lieber, is the most interesting task now available to anyone with my avocations" at which point the hammering had reappeared under Lieber's stubbled cheeks—Asher counterbalanced. But now the topology had been wrenched out of relation. With Benasseraf in his shallow grave, the finely spun poise and checks which had welded the hunting party were twisted. The cadence of the march, the maneuvers of survival had to be recast. Hence Simeon's question. Yes, the same question. But different now.

— I played Macduff. In the school production. All of whose family is wiped out by the fell kite—something like that, isn't it?—the dam and her chicks at one fell swoop. The hell-kite. That's it. It comes back to one. The boy who played Lady Macduff had a falsetto which could peel the skin off an apple. I remember his scream. Enter murderers.

Simeon spun around.

Teku had broken cover. The blowpipe over his shoulder was absurdly long, but he swung it with routine grace. He was moving toward the lean-to, his right hand outthrust. In it he held an offering, a strip of dried meat. The Indian went directly to where Hitler was standing, crooked over his own shadow. Teku bowed and placed his gift at the old man's feet. He knew that we must honor the old, and that the very old, like this bent man, are precious beyond topaz. "Ancient one," said Teku, "commend me to your spirits." And looked up warily. Thus saluted, Sr. Kulken had kicked him for his pains. But Kulken was garbage and a man must sometimes gamble. The parchment lips were making a magical motion. *"Blumen."* The Indian listened avidly.

13

(from the diaries of Blaise Josquin, Sous-secrétaire d'état *in the Political Intelligence section of the Palais Matignon)*

May 8th: Why do I flinch at my own detestation of disorder? When it has served me so well. When it has, in truth, been the mainspring of my career. Josquin *la règle*. Already in school. Then at the *École*. Where my desk drawers were the only ones in the entire *promotion* not overflowing with ash, paper clips, lozenges. Why the staleness now when more than ever, rigor is needed? Because nothing else, *mon vieux,* will throw any light into this muddle. I am bone-weary. It has been a bastard of a winter with R.H. ailing and "Attila" in a foul mood. Not that he rides me any more, not since the week-end at Rambouillet and the President's memo on my performance over the Libyan note. Bless E.F. I owe the old witch a lot. But it's more than just tiredness. Looking at myself in the mirror: *bonjour Seigneur Cliché.* The skull finely chiseled but not dramatic. The touch of silver at my temples. The fingernails unbroken. Everything as it ought to be: Anne-Estienne, our three children, the grange at

Lavergne, the beige coupé, my age and rank, these two high windows with south exposure reserved for those above the rank of assistant counselor. Every last orderly bit. *En place*. As it was on my night table when *Maman* came in to say "Good night *petit préfet*." Even V. But yesterday afternoon she was foul. I *wanted* to leave her. Listening to her high-class vulgarities (does she know what the words mean?), smelling her breath, I wanted to be back here, at my desk. Wanted it so much I would have given up the whole marvelous business in exchange for levitation. To be dressed instantaneously and float through the wall of that "little jewel" of an apartment. Which I've never had a taste for, but which she cherishes and now heaps full of her bric-à-brac. Perhaps *that's* why I'm feeling so down. "V. my dearest, *mon heure bleue*, perhaps it is time for us

May 11th: I have always resented Berdier. Since first we met at the seminar on fuel policies in Rotterdam. When was that? '64 or '5? The bluff exterior. The English worsteds, the Italian loafers. Another *cliché* figure. Down to the cork-tipped cigarettes and the new "atomic" lighter. God, he makes me sick. Because he's not like that at all. Underneath the talcum powder comes the sandpaper. Aphorism #3456 by the celebrated wit and moralist Blaise Josquin. Berdier is a brute, through and through. A gorilla. Should have been a bouncer or six-day bicycle racer. He is a crude killer. Probably was at some point in his meteoric ascent. *Who* is his patron? Not Ménestière. Too subtle, and a physical coward. Can it be P.? I was not at my best. Far from it. Berdier coming on strong and smooth. All that spurious deference to our department. He despises it. But we made an impression. Undoubtedly. "Attila" and his precious phrases about the "occasional need for direct, even unattractive methods of procedure." His annoyance at my "provisionality" (one of his favorite pieces of jargon). Who the devil wouldn't be "provisional" in the face of the evidence? And what evidence? That Semyonov has been seen arriving in Recife and has

137

been tracked as far as Manaus—*if* the identification is correct, at that distance across the airport and with a telephoto lens which Berdier himself qualified as not of the best? Hoving's visit? A nice young man & well trained. They order these matters in England. . . . But who could have been more tentative? "Ah that's the very point. Our Britannic friends are being *too* nonchalant. They must be on to something big, too big to share. . . ." I find Berdier intolerable when he puts on his Levantine airs. But there *may* be some merit to the point. At least "Attila" seemed to think so. And Hoving did seem to be holding back. But on what? Make a précis, Josquin; let the skeleton appear from under the skin, luminous. Not my idiom, but Follard's. The only great teacher I have ever been taught by. Great teachers are terribly rare. Killed in a road accident. Near Tarbes, trying to avoid a drunken motorcyclist. The skeleton, luminous. Oh God I am tired.

May 17th: No time for the diary. They want a protocol "gathering all the threads." A minute covering possible courses of action. Is there information I haven't been given? In which event only the President and the "inner cabinet" are in the picture. V. is sometimes oddly acute. It wasn't that xf was bad yesterday. On the contrary: explosive. But afterward she said: "Your body was fine today because it came alone. Your stuffed mind is elsewhere. Completely immersed in something. Good riddance." The tiny scratch above her nipple.

May 21st: Tocsins ringing. "Attila" having to give up his week-end. His face was a study. I had never seen General D. A legend in the Bureau and looked the part. Theroux set out the legal niceties. A brilliant memorandum. That youngster will go far. Now I have three days to pull the thing together, to weave the strands into a coherent pattern. What would F. have said: "Make of attention a closed fist, and remember that God lies in

138

the detail." He didn't make up that aphorism. I recall him telling us who had. I forget now. But what details have we?

What are our objectives? a) *if* it is Hitler, the Jewish organization must not be allowed to claim rights over his person, let alone transport him to Israel. Which had no status either *de jure* or *de facto* at the time of the said crimes or of the Nuremberg trials. Which, under the law of nations, cannot be considered a party to the case, though possibly a "friend of the court" or "interested observer" (point to be elucidated). Nor must he be handed over to the local authorities in view of the notorious tangle over extradition. Our American friends will probably attempt a snatch. Orosso (??) looks like the logical point of rendezvous and if the aerial photos can be trusted there is a light plane already waiting. But the strip looks totally waterlogged and we may have time. To what end? To arrive at a concerted policy along lines laid down at Potsdam. This is a four-power concern, precisely as is Hess's maintenance at Spandau. I can see Whitehall taking this obvious view. But what about Ivan? Our cables suggest that they are being bloody-minded, *per* usual: denying even the mildest interest in the story, while preparing what will undoubtedly be the most obstructive and divisive of attitudes. Our stance is plain & I see every benefit in stating it early. As cosignatory of the Four Power protocols, as one of the principals in the matter of indemnification and reparation for war crimes, the French Republic, via the legal agencies accredited both to the Nuremberg high court (have said agencies a successor, a continuing identity? Theroux was sketchy on this) and to The Hague, declares that etc. The venue for the hearings and actual trial? Delicate question. The European Court in Strasbourg! An inspiration, *vieux*.

b) But do we want a trial? If it is Herr Hitler—and why has Sir Evelyn Ryder come around to thinking it is?—the old devil must by now be a half-crazed scarecrow. The proceedings could turn farcical, and it is precisely our antennae for the ridiculous

139

which distinguish us from other nations. Even if the man they're dragging out of that jungle is still lucid, why open the old wounds? Things would get said, which all of us know and can, therefore, let be. That Vichy was not his creation, but a structure out of the heart of French history, out of an agrarian, clerical, patriarchal France which has never accepted the Revolution, which loathes the Jew and the Mason, which would, with a shrug, consign Paris to the devil. That to so many of my beloved countrymen—including my esteemed father and Uncle Xavier—it was the wrong war in the first place. "Perfidious Albion" and Jewish finance being the real enemies. On which point there was a queer unwritten concordat between Pétain and Le Grand Charles: both trying to preserve what they could of the French empire from British and American "liberations"—Madagascar, North Africa, the Antilles, St. Pierre and Miquelon. Vichy hoping Free France would get there before the "allies" and Free France anxious lest Vichy lose its grip too soon on Syria and Algeria. With all of which the *Reich* had precious little to do. And the larger design: a more or less united Europe, with strong central organs, from the Mediterranean to the Baltic, cemented by its fear of the Russian bear and of Asia beyond him, and embodying a United Kingdom cut down to continental size. Chancellor Hitler's dream and our current ideal, the very goal we are meant to be striving for. Drieux's testament; still worth reading. "Millions will have died through a hideous misunderstanding before Europe moves toward that unity which Fascism envisioned, that unity of the Teutonic-Latin genius in the face of the materialist barbarism of the United States and its grotesque imitator, the Soviet Union." Do we really want that stuff pouring out all over the front pages once again, reminding us of our grosser indiscretions? The mass killings—for that's what they were—at the time of the "liberation"? The betrayals before that? The years of the *milice,* no Germans in that bunch, and of the *French* camps?

c) But if he's not to be put on trial, what then? That, of

course, is where friend Berdier comes into the picture, he and his charming thugs in the *section spéciale*. Get to them first, says Berdier. And save ourselves immeasurable trouble and expense. "Pandora's box" said Berdier—his allusions are not recondite. "Let those crazy Jews and their find out of the woods and political nightmares will swarm." At which point the *Chef de Cabinet* listened. Too closely, I thought. "Special operations" are outside my competence. Not even "Attila" has to be informed. Perhaps the dossier I've been asked to prepare, Theroux's legal brief, the Minister's position paper are only a smoke screen. Berdier or someone even uglier could be under way now. I wash my hands of that. In any case, it would be political folly. The Americans must be there already. Four days without V., nearly five. I miss her, the smell of her instep, of the perspiration between her blunt fingers. But feel better than I have in months. More indifferent. It is soon midnight. "Attila" is waiting to see an outline of my report. Let him wait. I love my wife. She will believe me, she will know how deeply when we are older. Just how old would *he* be now? The "biography of the accused"—cretinous jargon—is here somewhere. April 20th 1889: which makes him exactly

May 25th: A shock last night when, as we were finishing supper, Edmond asked me whether I had ever seen Hitler. Had there been a press leak? The file is, of course, classified top security, but that means little nowadays. In fact, the boy had simply seen old newsreels being run on a television show, part of the waves of morbid nostalgia that now swamps film screens, television, bookstores. I had glimpsed the Führer once, at Montoire. Xavier had taken me along, as the most junior clerk in the *Maréchal*'s suite: "something to bore your grandchildren with, *mon petit*." We already knew that things had gone awkwardly at Hendaye, that Franco had been all smiles and not given an inch. *That,* surely, was the turning point in the war. Not Stalingrad, not Alamein, not, certainly, the landings. But the *Caudil-*

lo's refusal to let his precious allies and companions in arms have right of transit to Gibraltar. After which the Reich couldn't win. A classic war, really, a vintage European war over access to and control of Mediterranean routes. A problem ancient as Alcibiades' Sicilian debacle, and insoluble still. So our high guest was in a black mood. He lit up, momentarily, as would any tourist, on meeting the *Maréchal,* but the animation faded quickly. I watched him on the station platform, shuffling, bobbing about amid his staff—he rarely stood still—and stretching his legs during a break in the conference. I have a distinct recollection of a terrible tedium surrounding his person, streaming outward from him like a draft out of a cold sealed place. As if he were unspeakably bored, with his fame, with the machinery he had set in motion, with all the performances he would have to go through before an end whose futility he may already have intuited. I know this has a romantic, psychologizing ring to it. But I don't think I was fantasizing. The man was *ennui* incarnate. When he jerked into motion or rapid speech, it was obvious that he had tapped great springs of energy. But one supposed that these were somehow implanted in him, almost mechanically. The center was inert, probably lucid. Uncle Xavier said there had been a man just like that in his company, who had at some point early in the war imagined death with such hysterical intensity that he was never afraid again, merely empty and lashed on by occasional daring. How would he strike one now, after the years on the run? Has he wanted to survive or did that too "happen to him," coming from outside? How much does he remember of the giant, vacant thing he was? It *would* be fascinating to know, to hear that voice again. If Berdier gets there first, the occasion will hardly arise. If the Americans do, the psychologists will have their day. "The rehabilitation of Adolf Hitler; the elucidation of his childhood traumas." The triumph of the therapeutic. To Edmond the *Reichskanzler* is a figure out of the dim past, somewhere between the neolithic and the almost equally remote day-before-yesterday. Tarquin, Ivan the Terrible, Hitler, the Hundred Years' War—was it in Europe or in diverse unpronounceable parts of Southeast Asia?—all part of a school syllabus and television past. Totally unreal. Categorized for examination purposes or entertainment. If I had told the boy that Hitler was thought to be alive, that he might emerge on the box in the flesh, he wouldn't really have believed me. Is he wrong? I don't know myself. But this bizarre ghost-hunt *has* got under my skin. More than I realized. V. is fed up. Not with the hurried sessions and sudden cancellations (this is the first hour I've had to myself in ten days), but because she finds even my body "absent," "up the Amazon"—her oddly apposite turn of phrase. The affair will soon be spent. I know that, and don't mind very much, and don't know why I don't mind. This whole flap at the Ministry and the chance that I may soon be under way to South America (the presence of this branch is "quintessential" as "Attila" likes to put it) seem providential. Yes, that's the word. Providential. When I get back, Edmond must see a skin doctor. There is no reason for the boy to be disadvantaged. His mother has been so wrapped in herself lately. Or is it herself? I wonder, of course. *Bon soir Seigneur Cliché*. Why do I so hate disorder? Those memoranda folders askew on the shelf, when I have told my secretary a dozen times

14

— Do you believe me now, you dumb bastard? Well, do you?
Kulken had an appetite for abjection. Within limits. He also
had a flair for detestation. But his loathing of Marvin Crownbacker "call me Charlie" was of a disinterested purity, of a
constancy, which made him wonder. The stench of the man, of
his bare presence, choked him. Their intimacies had grown
manifold. That Crownbacker had moved in on him body and
soul, that he had taken his share of the Indian woman, that his
harsh mobile manner had electrified Orosso, these vulgarities
seemed to Kulken commonplace and vaguely fated. It was the
elusiveness in "ol' Charlie-boy," yet another of the tinny sobri-
quets his guest thrust upon him, that fixed Kulken's hatred, the
interleaving of grating banality—loud, caricatural, inescapable—with a strain dramatically contrasting. Just what the latter
consisted of was an enigma which gnawed at Kulken, kept him
off balance and hateful. He had, provisionally, settled on some
rubric tantamount to "authority"—to a covert, implausible yet
central authority. Whether of knowledge, clandestine rank or

solid purpose, he knew not. This ignorance, playing as it did on his nerves, had come on top of chaos.

First the airplanes: a jet of the Brazilian Air Force making two passes over the landing strip; then a light spotter aircraft racketing in at treetop level and circling Orosso in sluggish sweeps; next that dazzling job, a small commercial or company jet trying for a landing, twice, which was lunacy in view of the sodden, pockmarked state of the runway, then lifting away toward the jungle. With these incursions had come pandemonium on his receiver. A torrent of instructions, puzzling and otiose, from his employers, who demanded with shrilling impatience that the airfield (what an inflated name for it, thought Kulken) be drained and made ready, that a salubrious quarter (the blithering idiots) be reserved for "senior personnel," that Kulken, to whom a bonus was felt to be due, prepare to hand over. To all of which Kulken had, on Crownbacker's hoarse insistence, acquiesced, gaining time, gaining backbreaking nights in which to pick out of the air, drier now, lighter after the great rains, a gaggle of other voices. Many were in code, others sawed off by static and attempts at jamming. But some were plain enough. First they had crisscrossed the continent, weaving an imprecise grid, but then, as in an exercise in orienteering, they had zeroed in on Orosso, using his, Kulken's, transmitter as a focus. ("That, you poor crud, happens to be Russian"—one of Crownbacker's elucidations of the night before which had inspired in Kulken a particular jangle of worry and hatred.) It was merely the state of the runway—the winds had also savaged ol' Charlie's flying machine—which lay between Orosso and an outside world gone seemingly *loco*. But the margin of immunity was shrinking fast. Kulken had made out enough to know that bulldozers were at work, that the jungle track from Akonqui, the farthest point accessible to a Land-Rover, was being thrashed open. During bouts of fretful sleep he thought he could hear the distant falls of trees. It would not be long now. Only yesterday, through heavy mist, they had heard, or at least thought they had, the

145

clatter of a helicopter. A helicopter might land even now, though Crownbacker's plane was parked, oddly enough, across the center of the oozing strip. (Pounded with queries on just this point—"who the blazes is with you in Orosso, what's he come for, can you get his bleeding plane off the runway"—Kulken had omitted to answer, an omission the more decorous as Crownbacker, apparently indefatigable, hovered next to the splayed earphones, monitoring these inquiries with satisfied contempt.) But what now? What of their hopes, momentarily allied, once the mob poured in?

— What did I tell you, turd? What did Uncle Charlie tell you? Bormann . . . oh Jeeesus, don't make me laugh.

Hilarity, opined Kulken, was hardly on the agenda. He was, he felt, too finely honed to be taken in altogether by Crownbacker's sordid imaginings of bonanza. Nonetheless, if Herr Adolf did come mincing out of the bush *in propria persona,* and if Crownbacker-Kulken Wire Services Limited did have world rights, horns of plenty would gush. Characteristically offensive as the turn of phrase might well be, *amigo* Charlie's assurance that the event would "make that old epic on Golgotha look like a filler" had its grain of truth. But Kulken had ruminated further. The crass self-evidence of Crownbacker's design had left him restive. The strange beauty of this affair lay with politics, with the warp and weft of statecraft, with potentialities of international barratry or ransom to whose very existence Crownbacker appeared to be ludicrously obtuse. These filaments were Kulken's meat. He envisioned the sum of his past career, menace, humiliation and all, as a didactic prelude to this hour. Hold Hitler and the chancelleries would hop to one's piping. Not one but would have pressing grounds for direct or covert approaches, for competitive bidding. Washington, of course, and with immediate overreaching, lest Moscow get in first. London and Paris acting in concert at first, but soon at secret odds, laboring to meet Kulken's price. The two Germanys, almost by compulsive right. The Jews, both in Israel and abroad, to whom the prize

146

must, by now, be an indispensable talisman. It was less the money, though Kulken's sense of prodigality was material and far-flung. It was the commerce with high places, indeed the highest, the Byzantine delicacies of threat and cajolement, the savor of elevation above, of retribution on, the oily bastards who had in so many back rooms ridden him that filled Kulken's soul with vertigo, that made him breathe quick and deep as the earphones crackled.

But either eventuality—the richest carnival and scoop on record or the most arcane, remunerative of diplomatic imbroglios—required monopoly. Schickelgruber, alias A.H., must be safely in hand, his finders disposed of and the world kept at bay. The first two points lay in reach (Crownbacker had sounded the Indians and found them amenable to what would, after all, be a trivial ambush). It was item three which looked desperate. So many signals were pouring in, so many indices of feverish advance somewhere just beyond the horizon, that Kulken felt literally entrapped. How many more days before the pack barged in, high and mighty, scented with cologne and costly tobacco, thrusting Kulken aside, filching the credit, oblivious to the fact that it was he, Kulken, who had, by dint of tireless cunning, reeled in the leviathan out of the inviolate swamps? The injustice of it took Kulken by the throat and he half-rose out of his steaming chair. Crownbacker had also turned toward the door. The Indians stood there, three or four of them, brown as their shadows.

The jungle is strangely osmotic. Impenetrable in one sense, it is, in another, rifted by tunnels of communication. Explorers' postulates about totally isolated tribes, about corners of tropical forest or mountain innocent of any contact with the outside are largely spurious. Good shivery stuff for the glossy magazines, Kulken reckoned. Real isolation was formidably rare, if in fact it existed at all. How word sped across the barbed lines of mutually incomprehensible tongues, how iron utensils from the distant fringe stations came to be found in the inmost of the

Mato Grosso, was something of a riddle. But the facts were certain. News could tear like invisible fire through thicket and across cataracts. You had only to listen and it came humming back.

The party had been shadowed by Indians for at least a fortnight. Four white men with heavy loads, Teku and the Old One. They had been observed marching north-northwest, away from the shallow grave and toward the spur of the Cordillera. The ash of their night fires had been combed, their excrement pondered, their eviscerated food tins smelled and lifted to the light. The Cinxgu had communicated their notice to the Nambikwa, from whom the news had traveled down the Peranja, somehow arching the nine rapids, from where, in turn, the Jiaro had culled it for display in Orosso. Here it harvested fishhooks, lengths of rope, two bales of rough linen. So more news came. Of how the party was seeking to avoid the pass, now snow-blocked, and find a circumvention to the south; of how Teku appeared to be leading the actual march; of how he foraged for game. And now?

They had halted. Almost in sight of the mountains. They had been camping for several days, four, perhaps five. They no longer kept the Old One tethered. And Teku was carving a chair.

— A chair?

The Indians repeated the word.

Crownbacker did not wait for translation.

— Well, you dumb turd, do you believe me now?

Kulken reflected on the matter of the chair.

— Yes, he said,

— I believe you now.

15

— Marvin Crownbacker's red white and blue right down to his jockstrap. I'd take an oath on that.

— Maybe. But this is a lot bigger than anything he's ever been involved in. We should have sent a senior man, like Truscott. I was overruled.

— He's been doing fine up to now, Chief. He's a real broken-field runner, and that's what we needed. At least in the early stages.

— But who the hell is Rodríguez Kulken? The file stinks.

— I know, Chief, I know

It was hard to keep stride with the big man, in the crowded, interminable corridor that led to the press room.

— but he got there ahead of us. Johnny on the spot. Nine points of the law. And I'd be surprised if he'd blown Chuck's cover. Kulken's pretty small stuff. Just a stringer. Not even on the supplementary roster. I've got MI-6's word for that.

The Chief tired to snort audibly but the sound was lost in the hustle of feet.

— They were just lucky getting in there before we did. They took a chance. But Crownbacker's been in on the action almost from the word go.

The crowd was thickening and both men waved their passes.

— Let us through, please. 'Scuse me, ma'am. Okay, okay. Sorry. Coming through. No sweat, Sergeant, but just you keep that door closed once the Secretary begins.

The Chief had hefty shoulders, suddenly haloed by the blaze of klieg lights as they inched their way into the packed chamber.

— The whole goddamn mob. Just look at 'em. The Washington press corps. Pretty, aren't they?

— Well, Earl

The younger man was gripped by excitement, but immediately regretted his recourse to an informality which the Chief had often proffered but, no doubt, preferred to leave conditional.

— it is the biggest news break since

He was struggling for decisive analogy as the throng rose to its feet.

— Battle dress, muttered the Chief as he scanned the Secretary of State's alpaca suit and raw silk tie.

The voices and waving arms surged as from a sea anemone, bobbing impatiently.

— Ladies and gentlemen. Please. One at a time. Please.

— Riffler. *St. Louis Post-Dispatch*. Mr. Secretary, is it true . . .

The echoing buzz subsided slowly.

— I wish we could finalize our answer to that, Mr. Riffler, but we aren't absolutely certain. What I would say is this: on the basis of available evidence, and in view of the assessment made both by our own intelligence and that of the other sovereign states with whom we have been in touch, there is a reasonable expectation that the man found by what we understand to be— and I underline this point—an unofficial pursuit party is indeed the Head of State of the so-called Third Reich.

The voices and flash bulbs burst chaotically.

— Miss Marten. . . .

— Thank you, Mr. Secretary. Regina Marten, *Southern News Syndicate*. When do you expect Hitler to come out of those woods and who'll be there to receive him?

— Again, I'm afraid, the question is open to some doubt. According to the latest information we have, and you must realize, ladies and gentlemen, that communications from the heart of the Amazonian rain forests are somewhat circuitous

(Nice word that, thought the young man)

the party and the alleged Mr. Hitler have halted. South-by-southwest of Orosso, at the approaches to a high plateau beyond which our maps locate a native hamlet designated as Jiaro.

(The Secretary of State was glancing at his notes.)

Under optimal conditions the party could be expected to reach civilization, that is to say the airstrip and radio transmitter thought to be operative at Orosso, in something on the order of ten days. But I am given to understand that there have been early rains of exceptional intensity resulting in flash floods and fresh snow on the high places. As to the question of the status and identity of personnel at the presumed meeting point, I would prefer to reserve our position. As you can readily imagine, Miss Marten, this is an issue of extreme diplomatic nicety, involving as it does the local authorities as well as those foreign governments who may or may not have a valid claim to be regarded as interested parties.

— Escomb. *Time* magazine. Sir, do we have anybody on the spot, right now?

— You will understand, Bill, that it would be against the best interests of our government to go into details, at a moment when the relevant issues remain somewhat confused. But I think I could say this: the degree of surveillance we have been able to exercise over the day-to-day course of events should suggest to you that our position is one of readiness at both the local and global levels.

— Mr. Secretary, you've referred . . . sorry: Cord Dwyer,

151

Milwaukee Tribune. You've referred to contacts with other governments. Can you elaborate on that?

— Gladly. As is obvious to everyone concerned, the discovery of Herr Hitler, if identification turns out to be positive, is a matter for international response. The sovereign states party to the Berlin agreements and to the Nuremberg tribunal are naturally involved. So is Brazil, on whose territory the putative Reichschancellor was found and which he had, it is to be presumed, entered illegally. Since the time when the indictments for war crimes were drawn up, moreover, the political map has greatly changed. Both the German Democratic Republic and the German Federal Republic have declared their strong interest in the case. It is conceivable also that the Republic of Austria, in which the subject was born and, at different times of his life, domiciled, may wish to be a party to the proceedings of identification and to what are, unavoidably I fear, bound to be the intricacies of extradition. Though the issue is one on which our government has, as yet, evolved no firm view, there would appear to be a *prima facie* case for referral to the United Nations. I have instructed members of the United States delegation to solicit the views of the Secretary General and of his legal staff on this very point.

— What about Israel?

The voice was strained and the thick accent cut in above the chorus of questioners.

— Why haven't you mentioned Israel, Mr. Secretary of State? He's our prisoner, isn't he?

— Believe me, Mr. Simon—it is Mr. Simon, isn't it?

and the Secretary shaded his eyes for a moment against the hot banked lights.

— I would be only too pleased if I could give you an unequivocal answer. But our exchanges with your government on this entire matter have been less than satisfactory. It is no longer a secret to reveal that our first communications, transmitted as soon as expert opinion regarded the matter as potentially of substance, received nothing but routine acknowledgment. When we pressed for reply at a most senior level—the President himself has, of course, kept developments under daily review—the response from Tel Aviv was, to say the least, disappointing. So far as we are aware—and that comprises cables submitted to me this morning—your government has not taken any official note of the reports of Mr. Hitler's capture. It has neither acknowledged nor denied any participation in the recruitment, dispatch or future utilization of the search team. Inquiries on our part as to the position the State of Israel might take in respect of a possible trial before a multinational court have, hitherto, met with no clarification. So far as this Administration goes, efforts to elucidate and give the most favorable possible construction to Israeli concerns in the matter and to those of the Jewish community as a whole will, of course, continue.

— What if we get him out on our own, and transport him to Israel?

The same voice, hectoring.

— I would, I'm afraid, find it irresponsible to comment on so hypothetical a question. The precedent which you may have in mind, Mr. Simon, I refer to the Eichmann case, has, I feel, left a legacy of serious doubt with regard to international law and agreed usage among nations.

Out of the gaggle of voices an alto.

— Gene Jefferson, *Atlanta News-Times*. Mr. Secretary, in view of your previous answer, would you care to comment on whether or not a statute of limitations applies to Hitler's crimes. And what of the man's mental state? Suppose he is no longer fit to plead.

The Honorable Avery Lockyer dabbed his cheek.

— As many of you ladies and gentlemen are aware, I have spent a good deal of my life in the law. I am well aware of the fact that even at this considerable remove in time uneasiness over judicial aspects of the Nuremberg proceedings persists. This Administration and I personally hold no brief for special retroactive law. The ideal of common law precedents is enshrined in our way of life in these United States and, I would hope, in the policies of this Department. But you will recall that the statute of limitations was specifically voided with regard to what have been defined as "crimes against humanity." The current eventuality would appear to exemplify this category in an emphatic way. As to the issue of the accused's mental condition and degree of responsibility, it is obviously too early to express an opinion. I remind you that no identification has yet been validated nor any personal contact made by any agent of your Government. We would hope that thorough psychiatric checks can be initiated, under proper conditions, and as soon as possible.

— Tylden. AP. Do the Russians see it that way?

— I'd prefer to withhold comment on that, Ed.

— Mr. Secretary. Ann Carey. *Miami Herald*. Surely it would be possible to fly that party out. To pick them up by helicopter. Why all the delay?

(—Watch this, breathed the Chief, whose corner-of-the-mouth *sotto voce* was notorious throughout the service.)

— I wish it were that simple, Miss Carey. To the best of our knowledge the most proximate landing facility, at Orosso, has, until a few days ago, been waterlogged. Even from there, a helicopter pickup presents severe technical problems. It is, moreover, by no means evident what the attitude of the search party would be toward intervention at this point. Perhaps Mr. Simon would care to enlighten us.

Mild laughter in the stifling room and a shuffle of metal chairs.

— Big deal, muttered the Chief. Let's get back to the salt mine.

The younger man followed as they shouldered their way through the close-packed spectators and made for the exit. Just before they reached it and caught the cold draft from the now-empty

154

corridor, the young man registered an arresting voice, almost Gregorian.

— Sir, can you give us an assurance, an emphatic assurance, that due process will be followed and, most especially, that the accused will be given every legal aid for his defense?

Shutting the baize door behind them cut off the answer.

16

— Yes. But why me?

The antique banality. Its utterance submerged John Asher with leaden exasperation. For the very first time in the crazed meanderings of the entire enterprise, his heart gave out. The broken plain with its hummocks of saguaro, now in violent bloom, the rock abutments with their pale carpet of new snow went gray.

Elie Barach began his customary motion of persuasion and humble rapture, a miniature dance step back and forth. But Asher cut him short.

— I know. I don't really need an answer to that, do I?

— Friend Asher, you misconstrue. Do you know what the wisdom books say of the tribe of Aser, of your tribe? That they are a stubborn folk and sleep a serpent's long winter slumber. Who else can it be? Simeon has emptied himself, made himself a mirror so blank it no longer holds his own image. So that he can judge. I must read the Law, blessed be its Name. The boy Isaac? Since Gideon's death he is full of self-importance; grief has made him swell. It has to be my brother Jonathan. Who knows about fairness, and how they deem a man innocent until proved guilty, out there, in the real world.

Elie half-pirouetted toward the horizon, the little dance starting in his hollowed frame.

— In the real world. He reiterated the phrase.

And from just beyond the cliffs phantasms of a sane, populous existence seemed to tide across the fell.

The cry was in Asher's throat. But he said evenly

— I am no lawyer.

— True. True. Where there is a temple let the rabbi speak. Where there is only a rabbi let the unlearned hold their peace. Where there are ten simple men left, let them join in counsel. Where there is but one man left, let him be steadfast as the temple was, let him seek out the meaning of the Law as the rabbi did, let him take counsel with himself as if a score of just men inhabited his heart. We have only ash in hand to kindle a great fire.

And he set his fingers lightly on Asher's arm.

— He of Aser whose name is also in Manasseh.

— We don't have that far to go. They must be looking for us now. Perhaps Lieber is in Orosso already, or nearer. When we get out the thing can be done properly, as it should be. Elie we're play-acting and I'm sick of it.

Elie Barach, as to an obstinate child

— No. We've been through all that. A hundred times in these last few days. Since Gideon and the storms. By now those that are looking for us or waiting over the mountains are not ours. Simeon will hold out a while longer, but now he is like a tree in its last season. Rooted here. Move him and he will break. As for me, enough! "For I am ready to halt" says the Psalmist. Teku is as a sign sent us. To be a witness to the man's trial. An Indian guest come out of Eden to see the trying of one who sought to banish God, blessed be His Name, from creation.

— Out of Eden?

— Oh, I know. The stench, the bats, the leeches. But it is the nearest thing to the Garden left on the earth. By now men have wasted all the rest, pulping, scarring, dirtying the forests so as not to be reminded of that first Garden. But out here, there are instants

And Asher recalled the unnamed bloom, sultry gold and with leaves delicate as gossamer, which had shone before them at the edge of the swamps, or the silent rush of stars into the perfect concavity of the drumming lake, or the tenebra of a bird, out of sight in the canopies of high moss, the notes arrowing toward nightfall, velvet and swift. A guest out of Eden.

Teku had crushed a kada nut and rubbed the oil into the palm of his hand. Now he was giving a final polish to the carved legs of the ceremonial stool, sliding his fingers along the curved and spiraling motif which signified, in abstract yet unmistakable representation, the anteater sigil. Where his hand passed, the black wood glowed indigo. Teku had selected the heavy timber, testing the grain against his cheek. He had burnt the necessary hollows out of the living trunk and planed them to a lucent finish. The labor had to be perfect, for he knew himself to be watched. Not by the white men who walked like the blind, but by the Cinxgu and, now, by two Jiaro scouts well out of their own territory. At first, to be sure, the stalkers had done much to mask their presence. It had taken Teku several days and a nocturnal sweep of his own to be certain that the party was indeed being tracked, that each successive bivouac was being deciphered and culled for useful leavings. But in these last days, the watchers had dropped all but the most perfunctory pretense. A child would have made out the spoors of their approach to the edge of the encampment, the grass flattened where they had squatted, the russet traces left on the ground and leaves where they had chewed and spat. At moments they were so careless or scornful as to let themselves be heard. Four footbeats: a heavy man and his slighter companion. Teku had caught the sound just before dawn. None of his company had stirred. Deaf too.

He squinted at his art. Another pass with his flat hand and the wood shone back at the light of the early sun. It was a regal furnishing, a seat fit for an old man whose language Teku could not make out, whose skin sagged and splotched like that of a swamp rat three days gone, but in whose eyes the carver had seen two points of cold silver such as only the greatest of the tale-tellers, of the spirit-raisers possess.

Now he lifted the stool and carried it to the circle of swept earth, almost at the midpoint of the camp, as Simeon had ordered him to do. Let those Jiaro scarecrows gape. Let word of this throne travel as far as the nine falls.

Isaac Amsel could not take his eyes off this lambent handiwork. Uncertainly he slid his fingers over the subtly rounded seat. Teku's cunning, on the march, at food gathering, in the clearing of campsites filled him with troubled wonder. He had known of such skills, he had seen them acted in films of exploration and jungle romance. It was a different feeling altogether to witness them at first hand, adroitly enfolded, as it seemed, in the flesh of this small brown visitor, so brittle, so unprepossessing when compared with the stature of Benasseraf or that of Isaac's father. The Indian, in turn, prized the boy's endurance, the way he dogged and sometimes defied the older men. He was teaching him to handle the blowgun, to make of his pent breath a whistling rush, to spot the change of shadows behind shadows which signified game.

Elie had sat on the ground, halfway between the ceremonial stool and the seat Simeon had made for himself of an empty crate and gray blanket. For the first time since the capture, Simeon had unwrapped and opened the waterproof metal tube, so like a botanist's sampler, in which Lieber had stored the Articles of Attainder. He thought it would be best to read them aloud, then to give them to John Asher and the accused; after which he, Simeon, leader of the party and agent plenipotentiary, would set forth, with all deliberation and clarity, the grounds, reasons, motives which had caused him to institute proceedings here, at latitude x and longitude y, between the rain forest and the Cordillera, with himself as presiding judge. Elie Barach as explicator of the Law, Asher as defense counsel, and Isaac and Teku as witnesses. To state reasons for a procedure which ordinary good sense and world opinion would doubtless condemn as irregular, indeed mad, but which Simeon knew, upon searching examination, to be conclusive. In regard to the facts of the material and psychological reserves (now fast dwindling) of the party, in regard to their relation to the prisoner and the past, in regard to that indecent and piratical tumult which, they had every cause to expect, lay at the planned end of the march. Simeon had resolved to enunciate these propositions with condign solemnity. He had turned over in his mind phrases which, he knew, could be voiced this one and singular time only in human history. Elie had considered the pronouncement and suggested illustrative citations.

Now everything appeared to be ready. The accused was leaving the shelter with Asher at his heels. Simeon's mouth went dry as he waited for the two men to take up their appointed place. But already, as he came forward with his withered arm crooked to his side, Mr. Asher's client had begun to speak.

17

Erster Punkt. Article one. Because you must understand that I did not invent. It was Adolf Hitler who dreamt up the master race. Who conceived of enslaving inferior peoples. Lies. Lies. It was in the doss house, in the *Männerheim* that I first understood. It was In. God help me, but that was long ago. And the lice. Large as a thumbnail. 1910, 1911. What does it matter now? It was there that I first understood your secret power. The secret power of your teaching. Of *yours*. A chosen people. Chosen by God for His own. The only race on earth chosen, exalted, made singular among mankind. It was Grill who taught me. Do you know about Grill? No. You know nothing about me. Jahn Grill. But that wasn't his name. Do you hear me? Called himself Jahn, said he was a defrocked priest. For all I know he may have been. That too. But his real name was Jacob. Jacob Grill, son of a rabbi, from Poland. Or Galicia. Or. What does it matter. One of yours, yours, yours. We lived close. One soap sliver between us. It was Grill who taught me, who showed me the words. The chosen people. God's own and elect amid the unclean, amid the welter of nations. Who shall be chastised for impurity, for taking a heathen to wife, who shall have bondsmen and bondswomen from among the *goyim,* but stay apart. My promise was only a thousand years. "To eternity" said Grill; lo, it is written here. In letters of white fire. The covenant of election, the setting apart of the race, *das heilige Volk,* like unto no other. Under the iron law. Circumcision and the sign on your forehead. One law, one race, one destiny unto the end of the end of time. "And Joshua burnt Ai, and made it an heap for ever, even a desolation unto this day." "And Joshua made them that day hewers of wood and drawers of water for the congregation." All of them. Men, women, children. To serve Israel in bondage. But more often there was no one to enslave. "And they utterly destroyed all that was in the city, both man and woman, young and old, and ox, and sheep, and ass, with the edge of the sword." Your holy books. The smell of blood. Jacob Grill, friend Grill, and Neumann, for whom I painted post cards, they smelt of shit. But they taught me. That a people must be chosen to fulfill its destiny, that there can be no other thus made glorious. That a true nation is a mystery, a single body willed by God, by history, by the unmingled burning of its blood. It does not matter what you call the roots of the dream. A mystery of will, of chosenness. To conquer its promised land, to cut down or lay in bondage all who stand in its path, to proclaim itself eternal. "Let the trumpet blow in Zion. Let the Cherubim of the Lord bring fire and plague unto our enemies." You could hear the lice crack between Grill's fingers. God how his breath stank. But he read from the book. Your book. Of which every letter is sacred, and every mite of every letter. That's so isn't it? Read till lights out, and after, singsong through the nose, because he knew it by heart, from his school days, and had heard his father. The rabbi. "They utterly destroyed all that was in the city." In Samaria. Because the Samaritans read a different scripture. Because they had built a sanctuary of their own. Of terebinth. Six cubits to the left. They had made it seven or five or God knows.

162

Put to the sword. The first time. Every man, woman, child, she-ox, the dogs too. No. No dogs. They are of the unclean things that hop or crawl on the earth, like the Philistine, the unclean of Moab, the lepers of Sidon. To slaughter a city because of an idea, because of a vexation over words. Oh that was a high invention, a device to alter the human soul. Your invention. One Israel, one *Volk*, one leader. Moses, Joshua, the anointed king who has slain his thousands, no his ten-thousands, and dances before the ark. It was in Compiègne, wasn't it? They say I danced there. Only a small dance.

The pride of it, the brute cunning. Whatever you are, wherever, be it ulcerous as Job, or Neumann scratching his stinking crotch. You should have seen the two of us peddling those post cards, like starved dogs. But what does it matter if you're one of the chosen people? One of God's familiars, above all other men, set apart for His rages and His love. In a covenant, a singling out, a consecration never to be lost. Grill told me that. Jahn Jacob Grillschmuhl Grill or whatever his greasy name was, reeking of piss when he crawled up the stairs. Even he. The apostate. The outcast from Zion. Was still of the chosen, a private vexation to the Almighty. "Listen," he said, "listen Adi," no man else ever called me that, "you think you see me as I am, Grill the loser, the doss-house bum. But you're blind. All you *goyim* are blind. For all you know, Adi, I am one of the seventy-two chosen, chosen even above the chosen. One of the secret just ones on whom the earth rests. And while you snore tonight or swallow your spit, listen to me Adi, here in this barrack, right here, my blind friend, the Messiah may come to me and know me for his own." And he would roll his eyes and give a little laugh, a yellow Jew-laugh. It went through me like a knife. But I learned.

From you. Everything. To set a race apart. To keep it from defilement. To hold before it a promised land. To scour that land of its inhabitants or place them in servitude. Your beliefs. Your arrogance. In Nuremberg, the searchlights. That clever beaver

163

Speer. Straight into the night. Do you remember them? The pillar of fire. That shall lead you to Canaan. And woe unto the Amorites, the Jebusites, the Kenites, the half-men outside God's pact. My "Superman"? Second-hand stuff. Rosenberg's philosophic garbage. They whispered to me that *he* too. The name. My racism was a parody of yours, a hungry imitation. What is a thousand-year *Reich* compared with the eternity of Zion? Perhaps I was the false Messiah sent before. Judge me and you must judge yourselves. *Übermenschen,* chosen ones!

— What my client means, began Asher

Punkt II. There had to be a solution, a *final* solution. For what is the Jew if he is not a long cancer of unrest? Gentlemen, I beg your attention, I demand it. Was there ever a crueler invention, a contrivance more calculated to harrow human existence, than that of an omnipotent, all-seeing, yet invisible, impalpable, inconceivable God? Gentlemen, I pray you, consider the case, consider it closely. The pagan earth was crowded with small deities, malicious or consoling, winged or potbellied, in leaf and branch, in rock and river. Giving companionship to man, pinching his bottom or caressing him, but of his measure. Delighting in honey cakes and roast meat. Gods after our own image and necessities. And even the great deities, the Olympians, would come down in mortal visitation, to do war and lechery. Mightier than we, I grant you, but tangible and taking on the skin of things. The Jew emptied the world by setting his God apart, immeasurably apart from man's senses. No image. No concrete embodiment. No imagining even. A blank emptier than the desert. Yet with a terrible nearness. Spying on our every misdeed, searching out the heart of our heart for motive. A God of vengeance unto the thirtieth generation (those are the Jews' words, not mine). A God of contracts and petty bargains, of indentures and bribes. "And the Lord gave Job twice as much as he had before." A thousand she-asses where the crazed, boiled old man had had only five hundred to start with. It makes one vomit, doesn't it? *Twice* as much. Gentlemen, do you grasp the sliminess of it, the moral trickery? Cast your guiltless servant into hell, thunder at him out of the whirlwind, draw leviathan by the nose, and then? Double his income, declare a dividend, slip him a Lordly tip. Why did Job not spit at that cattle dealer of a God? Yet the holy of holies was an empty room, a silence in a silence. And the Jew mocks those who have pictures of their god. *His* God is purer than any other. The very thought of Him exceeds the powers of the human mind. We are as blown dust to His immensity. But because we are His creatures, we must be better than ourselves, love our neighbor, be continent, give of what we have to the beggar. Because His inconceivable, unimaginable presence envelops us, we must obey every jot of the Law. We must bottle up our rages and desires, chastise the flesh and walk bent in the rain. You call me a tyrant, an enslaver. What tyranny, what enslavement has been more oppressive, has branded the skin and soul of man more deeply than the sick fantasies of the Jew? You are not God-killers, but *God-makers*. And that is infinitely worse. The Jew invented conscience and left man a guilty serf.

But that was only the first piece of blackmail. There was worse to come. The white faced Nazarene. Gentlemen, I find it difficult to contain myself. But the facts must speak for themselves. What did that epileptic rabbi ask of man? That he renounce the world, that he leave mother and father behind, that he offer the other cheek when slapped, that he render good for evil, that he love his neighbor as himself, no, far better, for self-love is an evil thing to be overcome. Oh grand castration! Note the cunning of it. Demand of human beings more than they can give, demand that they give up their stained, selfish humanity in the name of a higher ideal, and you will make of them cripples, hypocrites, mendicants for salvation. The Nazarene said that his kingdom, his purities were not of this world. Lies, honeyed lies. It was here on earth that he founded his slave church. It was men and women, creatures of flesh, he abandoned to the blackmail of hell, of eternal punishment. What were our camps compared

165

with *that*? Ask of man more than he is, hold before his tired eyes an image of altruism, of compassion, of self-denial which only the saint or the madman can touch, and you stretch him on the rack. Till his soul bursts. What can be crueler than the Jew's addiction to the ideal?

First the invisible but all-seeing, the unattainable but all-demanding God of Sinai. Second the terrible sweetness of Christ. Had the Jew not done enough to sicken man? No, gentlemen, there is a third act to our story.

"Sacrifice yourself for the good of your fellow man. Relinquish your possessions so that there may be equality for all. Hammer yourself hard as steel, strangle emotion, loyalty, mercy, gratitude. Denounce parent or lover. So that justice may be achieved on earth. So that history be fulfilled and society be purged of all imperfection." Do you recognize the sermon, gentlemen? The litany of hatred? Rabbi Marx on the Day of Atonement. Was there ever a greater promise? "The classless society, to each according to his needs, brotherhood for all mankind, the earth made a garden again, a rational Eden." In the name of which promise tyranny, torture, war, extermination were a necessity, a historical necessity! It is no accident that Marx and his minions were Jews, that the congregations of Bolshevism—Trotsky, Rosa Luxemburg, Kamenev, the whole fanatic, murderous pack—were of Israel. Look at them: prophets, martyrs, smashers of images, word spinners drunk with the terror of the absolute. It was only a step, gentlemen, a small, inevitable step, from Sinai to Nazareth, from Nazareth to the covenant of Marxism. The Jew had grown impatient, his dreams had gone rancid. Let the kingdom of justice come here and now, next Monday morning. Let us have a secular messiah instead. But with a long beard and his bowels full of vengeance.

Three times the Jew has pressed on us the blackmail of transcendence. Three times he has infected our blood and brains with the bacillus of perfection. Go to your rest and the voice of the Jew cries out in the night: "Wake up! God's eye is upon you.

Has He not made you in His image? Lose your life so that you may gain it. Sacrifice yourself to the truth, to justice, to the good of mankind." That cry had been in our ears too long, gentlemen, far too long. Men had grown sick of it, sick to death. When I turned on the Jew, no one came to his rescue. No one. France, England, Russia, even Jew-ridden America did nothing. They were glad that the exterminator had come. Oh they did not say so openly, I allow you that. But secretly they rejoiced. We had to find, to burn out the virus of utopia before the whole of our Western civilization sickened. To return to man as he is, selfish, greedy, shortsighted, but warm and housed, so marvelously housed, in his own stench. "We were chosen to be the conscience of man" said the Jew. And I answered him, yes, I, gentlemen, who now stand before you: "You are not man's conscience, Jew. You are only his bad conscience. And we shall vomit you so we may live and have peace." A final solution. How could there be any other?

— The question the defendant is raising, rasped Asher

Do not interrupt. I will not tolerate interruption. I am an old man. My voice tires. Gentlemen, I appeal to your sense of justice, your notorious sense of justice. Hear me out. Consider my third point. Which is that you have exaggerated. Grossly. Hysterically. That you have made of me some kind of mad devil, the quintessence of evil, hell embodied. When I was, in truth, only a man of my time. Oh inspired, I will grant you, with a certain—how shall I put it?—nose for the supreme political possibility. A master of human moods, perhaps, but a man of my time.

Average, if you will. Had it been otherwise, had I been the singular demon of your rhetorical fantasies, how then could millions of ordinary men and women have found in me the mirror, the plain mirror of their needs and appetites? And it was, I will allow you that, an ugly time. But I did not create its ugliness, and I was not the worst. Far from it. How many wretched little men of the forests did your Belgian friends mur-

167

der outright or leave to starvation and syphilis when they raped the Congo? Answer me that, gentlemen. Or must I remind you? Some *twenty* million. That picnic was under way when I was newborn. What was Rotterdam or Coventry compared with Dresden and Hiroshima? I do not come out worst in that black game of numbers. Did I invent the camps? Ask of the Boers. But let us be serious. Who was it that broke the *Reich*? To whom did you hand over millions, tens of millions of men and women from Prague to the Baltic? Set them like a bowl of milk before an insatiable cat? I was a man of a murderous time, but a small man compared with *him*. You think of me as a satanic liar. Very well. Do not take my word for it. Choose what sainted, unimpeachable witness you will. The holy writer, the great bearded one who came out of Russia and preached to the world. It is sometime ago. My memory aches. The man of the Archipelago. Yes, that word sticks in the mind. What did he say? That Stalin had slaughtered *thirty* million. That he had perfected genocide when I was still a nameless scribbler in Munich. My boys used their fists and their whips. I won't deny it. The times stank of hunger and blood. But when a man spat out the truth they would stop their fun. Stalin's torturers worked for the pleasure of the thing. To make men befoul themselves, to obtain confessions which are lies, insanities, obscene jokes. The truth only made them more bestial. It is not I who assert these things: it is your own survivors, your historians, the sage of the Gulag. Who, then, was the greater destroyer, whose blood lust was the more implacable? Stalin's or mine? Ribbentrop told me: of the man's contempt for *us*. Whom he found amateurish, corrupt with mercy. Our terrors were a village carnival compared with his. Our camps covered absurd acres; he had strung wire and death pits around a continent. Who survived among those who had fought with him, brought him to power, executed his will? Not one. He smashed their bones to the last splinter. When my fall came, my good companions were alive, fat, scuttling for safety or recompense, cavorting toward you with their contritions and their memoirs. How many Jews did Stalin kill—your savior, your ally Stalin? Answer me that. Had he not died when he did, there would not have been one of you left alive between Berlin and Vladivostok. Yet Stalin died in bed, and the world stood hushed before the tiger's rest. Whereas you hunt me down like a rabid dog, put me on trial (by what right, by what mandate?), drag me through the swamps, tie me up at night. Who am a very old man and uncertain of recollection. Small game, gentlemen, hardly worthy of your skills. In a world that has tortured political prisoners and poured napalm on naked villagers, that has stripped the earth of plant and animal. That has done these things and continues to do them quite without my help and long after I, "the one out of hell"—oh ludicrous, histrionic phrase— was thought to have been extinct.

Asher's breath came loud and empty.

— Do not trouble yourself, *Herr Advokat*. I have only one more point to make. The last. That strange book *Der Judenstaat*. I read it carefully. Straight out of Bismarck. The language, the ideas, the tone of it. A clever book, I agree. Shaping Zionism in the image of the new German nation. But did Herzl create Israel or did I? Examine the question fairly. Would Palestine have become Israel, would the Jews have come to that barren patch of the Levant, would the United States *and* the Soviet Union, *Stalin's* Soviet Union, have given you recognition and guaranteed your survival, had it not been for the Holocaust? It was the Holocaust that gave you the courage of injustice, that made you drive the Arab out of his home, out of his field, because he was lice-eaten and without resource, because he was in your divinely ordered way. That made you endure knowing that those whom you had driven out were rotting in refugee camps not ten miles away, buried alive in despair and lunatic dreams of vengeance. Perhaps I *am* the Messiah, the true Messiah, the new Sabbatai whose infamous deeds were allowed by God in order to bring His people home. "The Holocaust was the necessary mystery before Israel could come into its strength." It is not I who have said it: but your own visionaries, your unravelers of God's meaning when it is Friday night in Jerusalem. Should you not honor me who have made you into men of war, who have made of the long, vacuous daydream of Zion a reality? Should you not be a comfort to my old age?

Gentlemen of the tribunal: I took my doctrines from you. I fought the blackmail of the ideal with which you have hounded mankind. My crimes were matched and surpassed by those of others. The *Reich* begat Israel. These are my last words. The last words of a dying man against the last words of those who suffered; and in the midst of incertitude must matters be left till the great revelation of all secrets.

Teku had not understood the words, only their meaning. Whose brazen pulse carried all before it. He had leaped up to cry out "Proved." To cry it to the earth twice and twice to the north as is the custom. But the air seemed to be exploding around him. Loud drumbeats hammering closer and closer, driving his voice back into his throat. He looked up, his ears pounding.

The first helicopter was hovering above the clearing. The second

—George Steiner